THE RUSSIAN INTERPRETER

Michael Frayn was born in London as a journalist on the *Guardian* and include *Towards the End of the M* *A Landing on the Sun*. *Headlong* was shortlisted for the 1999 Booker Prize, Whitbread Novel Award and the James Tait Black Memorial Prize for Fiction. His most recent novel, *Spies*, won the Whitbread Novel Award. His fifteen plays range from *Noises Off* to *Copenhagen*, and most recently *Democracy*. He has also translated a number of works, mostly from Russian. He is married to the biographer and critic Claire Tomalin.

Michael Frayn

The Russian Interpreter

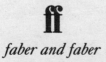

faber and faber

First published by Collins in 1966
This edition first published in 2005
by Faber and Faber Limited
3 Queen Square London WC1N 3AU

Printed and bound in Great Britain by
Mackays of Chatham plc, Chatham, Kent

A CIP record for this book
is available from the British Library

ISBN 0–571–22505–5

2 4 6 8 10 9 7 5 3 1

I

Manning's old friend Proctor-Gould was in Moscow, and anxious to get in touch with him. Or so Manning was informed. He looked forward to the meeting. He had few friends in Moscow, none of them old friends, and no friends at all, old or new, in Moscow or anywhere else, called Proctor-Gould.

All the same, Proctor-Gould was beginning to seem familiar. Chylde, at the Embassy, who sometimes used to invite Manning to the sad cocktail parties which he and his wife gave for the British community, had met him. So had one of the Reuters people, and Pylny, a walrus-moustached old man who edited an English-language propaganda sheet, and frequented Western visitors with dogged wistfulness. They all said that Proctor-Gould had large brown eyes, and kept pulling his ear as he talked. They would demonstrate, and try to recall him to Manning's mind, and as they demonstrated they would smile, as if the picture of him they had before their minds was somehow a little touching. They knew he was staying at the Hotel National and that he was in Moscow on business. But with none of them had he left any message for Manning to contact him.

He came closer. One morning Hurwitz said he had seen him. Hurwitz, a shambling bio-chemist from Czechoslovakia, had the room next to Manning in Sector B, the wing reserved for foreigners in the university skyscraper on the Sparrow Hills. He came into Manning's room in his pyjamatrousers, cleaning his teeth and spattering specks of toothpaste over Manning's walls and carpet.

'Saw an old friend of yours last night,' he said, his curious Czech Russian made more indistinct by bared teeth and toothbrush.

'Oh, yes?' said Manning. He and Hurwitz did not get on very well. Manning lived with almost fanatical tidiness, trying to create around himself a small stronghold of order in the vast confusion of Russia. Hurwitz and his habits were part of the confusion, and the two worlds overlapped disagreeably in the bathroom, which they had to share.

'He was at the desk here when I came in last night,' said Hurwitz. 'You weren't in, so of course they wouldn't let him through.'

He went out of the room, spat into the basin, and returned.

'He couldn't speak Russian,' he said. 'We tried in German, but he couldn't say much. Anyway, he asked me to give you this.'

He handed Manning a business card, now spattered with toothpaste and soggy from Hurwitz's wet fingers. On it was printed in Cyrillic characters:

Gordon Proctor-Gould M.A. (Cantab.)

Manning looked at it with distrust. Why did his old friend Gordon Proctor-Gould have a Russian visiting card? Why had he not written any message on it?

'I think your friend had something wrong with his ear,' said Hurwitz. 'He kept pulling it, like this – poum, poum.'

'Yes. Anyway, thanks.'

'There was a girl with him. He had his arm round her. She was crying.'

After Hurwitz had gone Manning sponged the spots of toothpaste off the carpet and set off for work. Gloomily, he walked along the miles of blue-carpeted corridors, down the triumphal staircases, and across the echoing marble foyers. The Proctor-Gould business was typical, he thought. Everything in Moscow was like this – unnecessarily complicated,

never more than half-explained. The simplest of l
rangements had to be heaved into place against th
tational pull of indifference and muddle. There were
two left shoes, and one finger too many to go in the holes
of the glove. He felt, as he often did, that he would like to
lie down, exhausted.

Outside, when at last he got outside, the complexity
increased. It was a brilliant day; the last of the snow had
melted almost everywhere. The mild, wet winter had col-
lapsed suddenly into the first marvellous warmth that sometimes precedes the spring. Manning felt suspicious; not even
the winters were unambiguous and straightforward.

He crossed the great empty plaza in front of the university, watched impassively by the gigantic gimcrack statues
thirty floors above of women grasping hammers and cog-
wheels. Everything seemed enormous and out-of-scale, like
one's fingers ballooning beneath one's touch in a fever.
Beyond the plaza, in the formal vista of the ornamental
gardens, solitary pedestrians moved like bedouin, separated
from one another by Saharas of empty brown flower-bed
and drying tarmacadam. They were so small they seemed
to be merely an infestation. The authorities should have put
human-being powder down and got rid of them.

He walked through the gardens. The air was mild. On the
marble benches here and there the old women gardeners lay
asleep in the sun, their rakes and forks propped up beside
them. Manning found the sight of them curiously moving.

There were more of them beside the little white church
at the far end of the vista, stretched out on the wet grass
itself. The church stood on the very lip of the high ground.
Beyond it, the grass slopes and birch woods dropped steeply
away, down to the great flashing silver arc of the river, and
beyond, as if caught and contained by that long meander,
the cathedrals, skyscrapers, parks, stadiums, and smoking
factory chimneys of Moscow. Manning gazed at it. God, it
was an intolerable city! And yet his feelings about it were

never entirely simple. On the river below two dazzlingly white steamers were passing each other in midstream. A train with a thousand trucks shunted slowly across the south of the city, puffing brilliant snowballs of smoke up into the sunshine. The evocative railway sounds came and went distantly in the breeze.

Manning thought of summer, and tears of longing pricked at his eyes. He thought of long journeys, and drinks at tables in the sun, and girls with white silk scarves over their piled hair, and slight cotton dresses over their delectable sunburnt bodies. He would go away somewhere. He would fall in love. Yes, this summer without fail he would have an affair with a sunburnt girl in a white cotton dress, who looked at him sometimes with troubled eyes, and held his hand against her face. . . .

2

A great morning for the comedians on the underground.

'Don't squeeze me like that, comrades,' begged a small man caught in the crowd that packed aboard the train at Frunzenskaya. 'I'm not an accordion.'

'For God's sake stop groaning, then,' said the large man who was pinning him against the doors.

Some days it was comedians. Some days everyone was reading serious books. Manning had to commute because he worked in one of the Faculties which had still not been moved out of the centre of the city for interment in that vast mausoleum on the Sparrow Hills. He had a brief moment of panic when his brief-case, which contained the precious fragments of his thesis, 'The Experience of Decentralization in the Administration of Public Utilities', became trapped on the far side of two more comedians, and was almost torn out of his grasp. It was a painful and frightening thought, which came to him from time to time, that the only tangible evidence for his eighteen months' hard labour in the city might somehow disappear before his eyes, like water into sand. It made him feel protective towards it. However unattractive it seemed, he would cherish it and feed it up and watch it grow to maturity. It looked like being his life's work. He had given birth to it at Cambridge, nursed it for a year at the London School of Civic Studies, brought it to Moscow for its health. But it was still poorly. Next year he would take it away to somewhere with a warm climate – Berkeley, perhaps, or Accra. It was a terrible burden, a sickly thesis. But when at last it had grown up and become a Ph.D. perhaps it would keep him in his old age.

He got out at Lenin Library, and walked up Mokhovaya Street into Manyezh Square, a vast parade ground without a parade. Tiny buses and taxis performed their evolutions in the sunshine, almost lost in the great distances. Flocks of pigeons fluttered, settled, and strutted about the central provinces of the asphalt plain, and beyond it the dark red walls of the Kremlin rose like a remote range of mountains. At the edge of these wastes the pavement was crowded. Authorized peddlars sold ice-cream, kvass, hot pies. A man in a stained blue suit tottered towards Manning, his arms hanging down, his eyes closed. He opened them at the last moment, saw Manning, and stopped. Then he took a pace backwards, side-stepped elaborately, tripped over the low wall in front of the History Faculty, and fell through the hedge. He stayed down, invisible but for his boots, which stuck out motionless over the pavement. No one paid any attention to him.

Manning turned up a narrow private alley between a postcard stall and a hot-pie concession. It led into a yard which was surrounded irregularly by the backs of buildings and occupied by two large wooden sheds and a stack of logs for the furnaces. Here the sun scarcely penetrated, and the walls were wet with long-stored winter moisture.

In one corner of the yard was a door, painted a blistered chocolate brown. The upper half of the door was glazed with dusty panes, and the small brass handle drooped ineffectually, worn loose and shiny over the years. Next to the door was fixed a plaque with old-fashioned gilt lettering on a shiny black background which announced:

FACULTY OF ADMINISTRATIVE-MANAGEMENT
SCIENCES

The sign was cracked from top to bottom.

Manning went in, and the heavy door slipped from his fingers behind him and slammed shut with a crash which rattled all the panes of glass in their crumbling putty. The inner door escaped from him, too, and crashed shut in its turn. In the corridor just inside was a sour-faced old woman sitting on a broken chair, her thick glasses askew, her hands tucked into her sleeves. Manning tried, as he always did, to walk straight by her.

'Pass,' she demanded, as she always did.

'You know me,' said Manning.

'I don't know anyone.'

Manning fumbled in his pocket, sighing to indicate his irritation. Once he had shouted at her each time he came in. Now he had been worn down to mere sighs.

'Someone came looking for you last night,' said the old woman, while she waited to find out who Manning was.

'An Englishman?'

'How should I know? He didn't speak Russian.'

'What did you do?'

'Chased him off. He hadn't got a pass.'

He showed her his university identity card, and walked up the bare wooden stairs to the first floor. The fourth, fifth, seventh, and eleventh stairs creaked as he trod on them. The building was alive with the quiet academic noise of Admin-Uprav at work. There was the uninterrupted monotone of one lecturer – Ginsberg, no doubt, on labour law; the little rushes and hesitations of another, Rubesh-chenskaya, the Professor of Social Statistics, who could never manage to work out her statistical examples on the board; the relentless, steady pulse of Korolenko, the Dean of the Faculty, giving his well-known lecture on the Essen-tial Attributes of the Soviet Administrator. There was the shuffling of feet on bare boards. Respectful laughter, need-ling laughter, and pervading everything, the Admin-Uprav smell, the weary, ancient smell of weak cabbage soup and greasy *pirozhki*, filtering up from the canteen in the base-ment.

Certainly I must get away, thought Manning. Perhaps I could afford to go to Finland for a few days? I wonder if they'd let me? He tried to recall the brownness of the limbs he had visualized on the Sparrow Hills, and the slightness of the cotton dresses which scarcely seemed to hide them. But they eluded him. There was no direct daylight on the staircases and in the corridors of Admin-Uprav. You couldn't have told that outside it was the first warm day of the year.

3

In the untidy little office on the first floor, beneath the portrait of Lenin with the brown stain gradually spreading outwards from the bottom left-hand corner, sat Sasha Zaborin. He looked up even before Manning was through the door, his quick, sensitive face already giving every pos-sible care and attention to whomever it might turn out to be. When he saw it was Manning he smiled. It was a warm, anxious, parental smile.

'Paul,' he said. 'You're late. I thought you were going to Romm's lecture this morning?'

'I went for a walk in the sun instead.'

'That must have been pleasant.'

'Yes. I'm sorry, Sasha.'

'There's no need to apologize to me, Paul. It was for your good I recommended it, not mine.'

'I know. I'm sorry.'

They spoke English together. Sasha spoke English at least as well as Manning spoke Russian, and he felt it was his duty to insist on putting himself out rather than the university's guest. He was a youngish man, only a few years older than Manning. He was tall, with a high forehead topped by a sparse crop of dry, dark hair which never lay down, and which had blown into a complex tangle in the wind on the way to the Faculty. There were lines of habitual conscientiousness at the corners of his eyes. He looked like a dark, anxious Eisenstein. It was easy, for that matter to imagine him wearing a cassock, and striding through some poverty-stricken parish surrounded by adoring small children. Manning sometimes called him Father Zaborin, a joke which he didn't much like.

'Anyway,' said Sasha, 'how's it going?'

'Not all that well.'

'No? What's wrong?'

Manning put his brief-case down and went across to the window. He gazed out at the familiar sight – a wall, streaked with long tongues of damp like dangling vegetation, bisected by a drain-pipe as wide as a dust-bin which dribbled continuously into the mud floor of a little courtyard. You could just see the blue sky if you put your face next to the glass and craned your neck round.

'I don't know. General dissatisfaction with life.'

'You're easily dissatisfied, Paul. But on a day like this, when you can almost feel summer in the air . . .'

'It brings it on.'

'Paul, you must realize that your dissatisfaction is not an objective phenomenon. It is a subjective state which you can control if you really want to. After all, a man is master

14

of himself. Remember Bazarov. "He who scorns his suffering inevitably conquers it."'

'And look what happened to him – he died.'

There was a silence, and Manning, turning from his study of the dribbling drainpipe in the courtyard, found that Sasha was gazing at him in a special worried way. He had suspected it.

'You're *concerned* about me again, aren't you, Sasha?'

'I can't help being a little anxious at times, Paul. I feel that these unconstructive moods of yours must affect your work. And naturally I feel that they are to some extent a reflection on myself.'

'Now, Sasha, don't start all that again.'

'I know it's not entirely easy, living in a foreign country. It's up to me to make you feel happy here.'

'That's the trouble, Sasha. It's not up to you – it's up to me. All you have to do is leave me in peace, and not fuss, fuss, fuss around all the time.'

'Paul, you were feeling out of sorts when you walked through that door!'

'Well, now I'm feeling worse.'

Sasha went on gazing anxiously at Manning. Then he smiled.

'I prescribe more relaxation. I'll get us some seats for the theatre.'

Manning felt like a spoiled child. He would have liked to stamp his foot.

'I don't want to go to the theatre,' he said. 'There's nothing but rubbish to see.'

Sasha was hurt. His whole face tensed for a moment before, as Bazarov recommended, he scorned his suffering and mastered it, and forgave Manning. He was always hurt by Manning's contempt for national institutions of which he had been taught to be proud. Once he had been unable to bring himself to speak to Manning for two days because Manning, irritated by some skirmish with the bureaucracy, had told him that pigs were treated with more respect in England than men in Russia. In the end, his eyes full of a special bewilderment with which he sometimes softened the pain, he had told Manning: 'It's just not true, Paul. In the Soviet Union a man feels he is *needed*, which is the greatest respect that anyone can be paid.'

Now he suggested a concert.

'I don't want to go to a concert, either,' said Manning. 'I want to get away from Moscow for a bit.'

'All right. I'll organize something. Perhaps we could go to Zagorsk again. Or if the weather stays as warm as this it might be possible to take a picnic up the Oka.'

'I want to get right out of the country. I want to go to Finland for a week.'

'What – now?'

'As soon as possible.'

'I don't know whether that could be arranged, Paul. Why not wait until the summer vacation? I don't know what the committee would say about your leaving the country now.'

'You could ask them.'

'Yes.'

'They'd do whatever you recommended. You could let me off the leash for a bit.'

Sasha looked more anxious than ever.

'You see, Paul,' he said, 'I'm personally responsible for you to the committee. I'm responsible for seeing that your research goes well while you are in our country. Now, it's not true to say that I keep you on a leash. You are perfectly free. I ask only that you give me some account of where you have been, and that you consult me before you make any major trips. Isn't that the truth?'

It was close to the truth. Manning let his annoyance expire in a long sigh. It was very difficult to complain of the way Sasha treated him. He felt ashamed of himself for returning all Sasha's kindness and thoughtfulness with ungrateful petulance.

'As a matter of fact,' he said gloomily, looking out of the window again, 'I haven't got enough money to go to Finland just now, anyway.'

Sasha was silent.

'I'm sorry, Sasha,' said Manning.

'If you do decide you want to go,' said Sasha, 'I'll certainly ask for you.'

'No, no. It was just one of those ideas one has.'

'I only want to do what's best for you, Paul.'

'I know you do. I'm sorry.'

Sasha's gentle eyes rested on Manning, full of earnest sympathy.

'I know the feeling, Paul,' he said. 'A great restlessness. I get it too on a day like this. I'll tell you what we'll do. We'll go to the Conservatory this evening. My friend Yuri Shchedrin – I told you about him; we used to play duets together when we were boys – is singing twelve Schubert songs. We'll forget our troubles. We'll forget Soviet public utilities. We'll forget Moscow.'

Excited, as he always was by the sound or the thought of music, he began to sing 'Frühlingsglaube' in his sweet, soft tenor.

'*Die linden Lüfte sind erwacht . . .*'

'That would be nice,' said Manning.

'And afterwards we could go on to that Georgian grill in the Arbat. Have a *shashlik* – drink a bottle of wine – look at the pretty girls.'

'I look forward to it,' said Manning. And suddenly he did. He felt unable to look beyond the prospect of small pleasures in the immediate future, as if he were a child. In various pleasant or unpleasant ways Sasha often made him feel like a child. He picked up his bag and went to the door.

'I apologize for my childishness,' he said.

Sasha waved the apology away.

'Incidentally,' he said as Manning opened the door, 'I hear there was someone round here looking for you last night.'

'So the doorkeeper told me.'

Sasha looked at him expectantly. When Manning did not elucidate further, he asked:

'That would be your friend Gordon Proctor-Gould, would it, Paul?'

'Would it?'

'I thought it might be. I believe he's trying to get in touch with you.'

'You've met him, have you?'

'No, no. I heard about him.'

'From whom?'

'From some friends of mine. You'll be in the library, will you, if he calls again today?'

'Yes.'

'Perhaps I could invite you both out for dinner some time? You know I'm always pleased to meet any friend of yours, Paul.'

'Yes,' said Manning. 'I know.'

'Particularly a very old friend like Gordon Proctor-Gould.'

'Quite. You're not the last person in Moscow to meet him, Sasha, I assure you. I've never set eyes on him myself.'

Manning shut the door and walked down the corridor towards his habitual place in the Faculty library. He already felt slightly guilty. Sasha would worry about Proctor-Gould now all morning.

4

Another diamond-bright day was ending. Luminous shadows reached across the great central squares; devoured them entirely; left only the skyscrapers still shining in the pale gold light.

By the fountains in Sverdlov Square Katerina was already

waiting for Manning, darting little nervous glances about her like a bird. She was still wearing her winter overcoat and her brown woollen stockings. Beneath the blonde plait looped up around her head her face was all pink-and-white – a winter face. She saw Manning while he was still crossing the roadway, and ran to meet him between the traffic lanes, putting her hand on his arm for a second and giving him a quick, shy smile.

'You look so tall and dark and discontented,' she said, letting him watch out for the traffic and guide her by the elbow. 'You must learn to accept yourself.'

'It's the circumstances around me that make me discontented.'

'The circumstances around you are part of you. People carry their lives about with them like tortoises carry their shells.'

Manning found the grave aphorism a solace. Though he supposed that she might equally well have said: 'One's circumstances are insignificant. People shed their lives like snakes slough their skins.' He supposed he would have found that equally comforting.

They began to walk about the city, at a steady pace but in no particular direction, companionable but not touching each other, and for some time saying nothing. They left the crowded pavements of the centre, and lost themselves in streets fronted by peeling brown apartment blocks, and small basement workshops whose pavement-level windows exhaled heat, clatter, and the smell of oiled machinery.

Manning thought that Katerina was somewhat younger than himself, but he did not know. He knew very little about her or the life she carried around with her; they never talked about such things. He didn't even know where she lived. He wrote to her by way of a box number in the Central Post Office, suggesting a meeting-place. Then they would walk the streets for an hour or two, sometimes talking, sometimes silent.

'Look up at the sky,' she said. 'Blue and gold from horizon to horizon. Now you're looking into the iris of God's eye.'

'Literally, Katya?'

'Oh, yes. The sky *is* God's iris. But it is also God's sadness, and God's great age. All God's attributes are every part of Him.'

'And yet I've heard you say, Katya, that God is within us?'

'Yes – He within us, and we within Him. We *are* God, Paul.'

'But we're free to please or displease Him.'

'Of course. We are entirely free in every possible way. But our liberty must be comprehended in God's Liberty. That's obvious.'

Katerina often talked about God. She had apperceptions of Him at every corner, feeling His presence in the air she drew into her lungs, seeing His hands pierced by the skyscrapers. Manning liked to hear her speak of God, and led her on with questions. He liked to think of the hot lathes in the basement workshops and the inert masonry of the public buildings as being in some way impregnated with human attributes and sensibilities, just as he liked to try to see the whole visible world, including himself, Katya, and the people crowding off the trolley-buses on their way home from work, as nothing but a complexly interbalanced network of electrical charges. It was an astonishing vision – like suddenly catching a glimpse of oneself from behind in a double mirror.

'As you know,' he said, 'I don't understand what you say about God at all.'

'Nor do I. We couldn't expect to. All we can do is to venture descriptions of Him which give rise to unfathomable infinities and unresolvable contradictions, and to contemplate these with humility.'

Sometimes Katerina spoke of the sufferings of people she knew, particularly those of her friend Kanysh, who had remained in Moscow for a year without police permission in order to be near her, unable to get a job because he was a Kazakh. He had been in despair and ill with hunger, and he had been deported to Ulan-Bator back in November, just before Manning had met Katerina at the door of the Foreign Literature Library, weeping because she had forgotten her pass and couldn't get in. Katya collected Kanysh's letters from Box Number 734 at the Central Post Office and read them as she walked about the streets. Manning had seen her. The letters were written in a close, sloping hand on thick wads of cheap blue writing paper, and she carried them round and re-read them until they wore out at the folds and fell to pieces.

How Katerina supported herself Manning didn't know. He believed she lived with a widowed mother and an aunt, and that she had some connexion with the Philological Faculty. He felt it would have been overstepping the boundaries of their relationship to ask. He knew that she was translating Rilke's *Geschichten vom lieben Gott* into Russian. But of course, it would never be published. He had no idea how far she had got with it. Sometimes her remarks seemed to indicate that she was revising a finished translation. Sometimes she seemed to suggest that it was beyond her even to start.

They walked down a long, straight avenue with factory chimneys smoking behind blind brick walls. The street-lights sprang on in the thickening dusk.

'Shall I tell you a story?' asked Katerina.

'Yes, I'd like to hear one of your stories.'

She thought for a moment.

'In a far distant land,' she said, 'there lived an old man with three sons. The old man was dying. He called his three sons around the bed and told them he had one last wish – to see before he died a man who had led a life of perfect happiness. So the three sons set off to search the world for such a man. The eldest son, Petya, searched the cold lands in the north. The next eldest son, Kolya, searched the hot lands in the south. And the youngest son, Vanya, took a boat and searched the Empire of the Sea-King. . . .'

5

Later they talked about Sasha.

'I wish he'd lose his temper with me when we have these scenes,' said Manning. 'He just looks hurt, and then forgives me.'

'It's better to hurt someone who's capable of forgiving you than someone who's not,' said Katerina.

'It doesn't seem like that at the time.'

'There's no point in having moral qualities if they're not used.'

'That sounds cynical.'

'It's not intended to be.'

'But, Katya, you wouldn't want me to hurt your feelings, just so that you could exercise your forgiveness?'

'No, because I'm not strong, like Sasha. I'm weak, and I shouldn't forgive you.'

They walked in silence for some minutes.

'He took me to hear Shchedrin last night,' said Manning. 'He knows him – they were in an orphanage together during the war. We had dinner with Shchedrin and his wife afterwards.'

'Did you like them?'

'Yes, I did.'

'Was Shchedrin very modest? Did he make little jokes in a quiet voice, and make everyone laugh respectfully?'

'Do you know him?'

'No, but I can imagine him. A neat blue suit. A tidy, quiet face, with smooth skin filling out a little round the jowl.'

'That's a caricature. . . .'

'No, it's a description. All Sasha's friends are of a type.'

'You've never met Sasha or his friends.'

'You've told me about them. I know their sort.'

'Their sort? Katya, why are you so contemptuous of them? They're good people.'

'Of course they're good. They're strong, good, able people, whose strength and goodness and ability enable them to rise above their brothers. Well, God be with them. But I want to make it clear that I am one of the others – the ones who are not strong or good enough – the ones who are risen above.'

'Sasha and Shchedrin may be better paid. . . .'

'It's not money, of course. Even if Shchedrin had to walk the roads and beg his bread, he'd still know that he could sing like one of God's angels. That would be real riches.'

'And you want to take that away from him?'

'No! I just want to commit myself to those who have no such riches. That's the real battle in life – the one between the strong and the weak.'

'And you're weak, Katya?'

'Yes. I'm weak because I'm afraid of so many things. But I recognize my weakness, and I use it as my passport to where I want to be – in the ranks of the losers.'

'Am I weak, Katya?'

'Oh, yes. But you'd never admit it to yourself. You'd like people to think you were strong. So you put a good face on it and stay close to those who are strong – like a little boy who marches down the street with the soldiers.'

It was quite dark, and suddenly very cold. The feeling of spring had gone with the light.

'I met someone last night,' said Katerina after a long silence, 'who said he was an old friend of yours.'

'Proctor-Gould? Where did you come across him?'

'At the desk in Sector B. I came to look for you.'

'Oh,' said Manning, 'it was you?'

'The woman at the desk wouldn't let me in, and she

wouldn't tell me whether you were there or not. So I started to cry – you know how I do.'

'Then Proctor-Gould came along?'

'Yes. He tried to cheer me up. He spoke a little German – very badly.'

'What did you think of him, Katya?'

'I'm not sure. I thought for a start that he was very confident – he put his arm round me as if it was the most natural thing in the world. But then I began to wonder if he wasn't one of those people who do everything boldly and confidently in order to impress themselves – to convince themselves by external evidence that it must be right. It's like trying to persuade oneself one's rich by spending money – a sort of confidence trick upon oneself. One day the bills fall due and one discovers one's own deceit.'

Manning looked at his watch. They had been walking for over an hour.

'Shall we find a restaurant and have something to eat?' he asked.

Katerina shook her head.

'One can't talk and eat. Anyway, two people can't really talk facing each other. It's much better to talk in the streets, walking side by side.'

'Do you want to go on walking for a bit, then?'

'No. There's nothing more I want to say to you today. Good-bye, Paul.'

For an instant her head turned towards him, her nervous smile flickered in the light from the street-lamps, and her hand rested on his arm. Then she had turned and was disappearing down the steps of a Metro station. Manning gazed after her, disconcerted by her lack of ceremony and shocked by her frankness.

The station was called Komsomolskaya, after the Communist League of Youth. He stared at the word, aimlessly repeating the melodious syllables over to himself. Behind him someone cackled with laugher, and shouted out:

'You look, and look, and look!'

Manning swung round. For a moment he could see no one. Then there was another burst of laughter from somewhere down near pavement level, and Manning saw an old man with snow-white hair, sitting propped up in a little wooden trolley, like a Guy Fawkes in a go-cart, with leather pads on his knuckles to push himself along. Both legs were amputated just below the groin.

'You stare, and stare, and still you stare!' cried the old man, leaning on his padded knuckles and shaking all over with violent laughter.

6

In the end Manning met Proctor-Gould by chance. He was walking past the Hotel National after lunch one day when a man with a large, lugubrious face came slowly out, gazing absently at the street with eyes as soft as a spaniel's and pulling at his right ear. He was wearing a double-breasted blue blazer with brass buttons, some sort of institutional tie, and dark grey flannel trousers. His breast pocket was full of pens. His suède shoes were going shiny over the bulges made by the little toes, and there were odd threads of cotton adhering to the nap of the blazer. Manning was astonished. Why had no one mentioned that he was moon-faced? Or that one's overall impression of him was one of seediness? But he did not doubt for a moment that it was Proctor-Gould.

As he drew level the sad brown eyes focused on him.

'Paul Manning,' said Proctor-Gould conversationally.

'Gordon Proctor-Gould,' said Manning.

They shook hands, as if they really were old friends, and had not seen one another for a month or two.

'I've been trying to contact you,' said Proctor-Gould.

But you seem to be rather an elusive customer.'

'Why didn't you leave a note for me and tell me where you were staying?'

Proctor-Gould gave a wry chuckle.

'I did think of it,' he said. 'The old brain will just about run that far. But let me confess, I thought I'd take the opportunity to meet some of your friends and find out a little about you.'

He looked at Manning, his eyes open humorously wide, inviting Manning to register some sort of humorous indignation in return. Manning felt that he would have been most at home in one of those conversations which consist in the leisurely exchange of heavy banter, like the desultory dialogue of long-range artillery. There was some sort of ponderous charm about him. Manning saw why people smiled when they thought of him.

'Naughty of me, I know, Paul,' went on Proctor-Gould, pulling at his ear again. 'But one learns to make a few discreet inquiries about one's potential business associates.'

'I'm a potential business associate?'

'I have a little proposition to put to you. Can you spare ten minutes now? We could talk about it over a cup of coffee.'

Manning nodded, and Proctor-Gould ushered him into the gloomy lobby of the hotel, where only the polished brass fitments and the pale suits of American tourists gleamed among the sombre pre-Revolutionary furnishings.

'It makes a change to be dossing down in this place,' said Proctor-Gould. 'They usually put me in the Hotel Ukraine, miles from anywhere. I seem to be *persona* fairly *grata* with the authorities at the moment.'

They went up to Proctor-Gould's room, a dark, lofty chamber on the third floor, furnished in the characteristic Imperial baroque, and looking out over the Kremlin. Proctor-Gould appeared to be not so much occupying the room as camping in it, like a rambler in some corner of the lawns at Versailles. An open suitcase lay on the floor at the foot of the bed, a tangled heap of possessions straggling out across the carpet. Suspended on plastic hangers from the dark furniture all about the room were wet shirts and socks, dripping into antique ornamental bowls or on to pages from Soviet newspapers.

'I'm sorry about the laundry,' said Proctor-Gould. 'But I don't trust the local washerwoman not to boil and beat my shirts to pieces. Sit down and make yourself at home.'

He rummaged in the suitcase, found a little aluminium camper's kettle with a folding handle, and disappeared with it into the corridor. Manning sat down in an uncomfortable carved chair, with brass lions' heads beneath his hands, and gazed about him, steeping himself in the profound melancholy of the room. On a table in the corner were stacked dozens and dozens of English books, all still in their dust-jackets. Manning put his head on his shoulder to read the titles. He made out *Religion and the Rise of Capitalism*, *The Human Use of Human Beings*, *Philosophical Investigations*, five copies of *Lucky Jim*, and seven copies of the *Concise Oxford Dictionary*.

'I see you're looking at my beads,' said Proctor-Gould, coming back into the room holding the kettle, now steaming, at arm's length.

'Your what?'

'My beads. Presents for the natives. I always bring a suitcase full of English books when I come over – they're like gold-dust here.'

He felt under the clothes in his case again, and produced two stout plastic mugs. Inside a spare suède shoe he located a Woolworth's apostle spoon, and beneath a pile of dirty socks the old familiar tin.

'Do you mind Nescafé?' he asked.

'Delightful.'

'I always bring it. Boiling water's the only thing you can get without waiting in Russian hotels.'

Manning watched him lever open the lid with the apostle's head, and perform all the rest of the soothing ritual. It took him back. It took him back to all the indistinguishable student lodgings in which he had sat, beneath mantelpieces lined with the annual programmes of university societies, and party invitations all written on identical At Home blanks as if they were impersonal communications from some university department responsible for partygiving. To evenings spent talking about women and grants to visit America, and consuming chocolate digestive biscuits and Nescafé, the body and blood of scholarship itself. Nostalgia touched him, and he felt pleased to be with another Englishman here amid the sad smells of Russia.

'You'll have to have it black, I'm afraid,' said Proctor-Gould, though the liquid in the mug was more a kind of dark gravy brown. 'There seems to be a milk shortage in the shops at the moment.'

'Thanks,' said Manning. 'It's nice to meet you at last. I hear we're old friends.'

Proctor-Gould took his own mug and straddled comfortably with his back to the radiator, as if it were an open fire. He gazed benignly down at Manning.

'We are, Paul,' he said. 'We are.'

'Really?'

'You don't remember where we met?'

'No.'

'At John's.'

'John's? John who's?'

Proctor-Gould laughed. It was a snuffling laugh, the kind of noise one might have expected a bloodhound to make, if something about the scent had struck it as funny.

'"John who's?"' he repeated contentedly. 'That's good. I must remember that.'

'I still don't know.'

'We were in college together, Paul.'

'Oh, *John's*.'

'It's not what he says,' said Proctor-Gould, in great good humour. 'It's the way he says it. Anyway, I've been checking up. You were two years behind me. But I'm pretty sure I remember seeing you around in my last year.'

'Now you mention it,' lied Manning politely, 'I rather think I remember seeing you.'

'You had a room in Chapel Court, didn't you?'

'I didn't, as a matter of fact.'

'Ah. I probably just saw you walking through.'

'That would explain it.'

'But we must have seen one another in Hall, for example.'

'Of course we must.'

It was presumably a John's tie that Proctor-Gould was wearing. Now that Manning had a reference point against which to locate him, Proctor-Gould appeared even more curiously seedy. Double-breasted blazers and baggy grey flannels had gone out of fashion years before he and Proctor-Gould had arrived in Cambridge. Vaguely he visualized a Cambridge full of perambulating double-breasted blazers just after the war, with utility marks in their linings and ration books in their pockets.

'Anyway,' said Proctor-Gould, 'I'm in business now. You see before you one of the bright young men you're probably always hearing about who go out and develop trade with the Soviet Union.'

He smiled lugubriously, and pulled vigorously at his right ear – with his left hand this time, since he was holding the mug of Nescafé in his right. When he stopped, Manning noticed with a shock that his right lobe was visibly longer than his left.

'What do you deal in?' asked Manning.

'Oh, pictures, fashions, musical instruments – all the little unconsidered trifles that no one else thinks of as coming from Russia. And people.'

'People?'

'Yes, quite a large proportion of my business is in people.

I expect you'll think that means I'm a theatrical agent?'

'I can't think what it means.'

'It's a conclusion a lot of people seem to leap to. But in fact I don't touch the theatrical profession at all. I'm not a literary agent, either – that's another common mistake people make. I don't handle authors, in the normal sense of the word.'

Proctor-Gould gazed thoughtfully into the brown dregs of his Nescafé, as if brooding upon human error and delusion.

'No, Paul,' he said, 'I deal exclusively in ordinary people – the more ordinary the better. And this is where I want you to help me.'

7

'The point is,' said Proctor-Gould, 'there's a tremendous demand for ordinary people. The Press and television in Britain and America are crying out for good human material. You might think it's strange at first sight, but producers and editors find it very difficult to meet people outside the entertainment industry. They simply don't come across them. It's easy enough for them to get hold of professional personalities, of course – novelists, pop singers, beauty queens, politicians, that kind of person. But they want to get away from the professionals. They want to get at the real flesh-and-blood people who make up the other 99·9% of the world. There's a market all right. And of course there's a plentiful source of supply. All you need is a middleman to bring the two together.'

He put his mug down, warmed his hands at the radiator behind his back, raised himself on his toes, and let himself sink slowly back on to his heels again.

'I hope I don't sound mercenary,' he said. 'For me this isn't just a way of making money, I assure you. It's something I believe in very deeply. You see, Paul, I think professional personalities aren't the only interesting people around. I believe that *everyone* is of interest to the public. I believe that *everyone* has a story to tell, a point of view that's worth putting across, a personality that the public would be interested to explore.'

He hesitated, and smiled anxiously.

'I don't know whether that seems just a lot of absolute balls to you?' he asked.

'No,' said Manning. 'Oh, no.'

'It seems a lot of absolute balls to some people.'

'Really? Not to me.'

'No, well, it doesn't to me, of course. But I know from experience that it does to some people.'

He picked up his mug again, and ate a spoonful of the syrupy, half-dissolved sugar at the bottom.

'I said that everyone is of interest. In theory that's perfectly true. But time and human patience being limited, in practice one has to select only people who can put themselves across. That's why a skilled agent is needed. That's what I earn my modest margin for.'

'How do you tell who can and who can't?'

'It's a knack, Paul. It's just one of those funny old knacks. I can tell within a few minutes of meeting someone whether they're suitable or not. For instance, you're not, if you don't mind my saying so. You wouldn't come over at all.'

'I'm sorry.'

'No need to apologize. It's not something you can control. It's like being pigeon-toed, or colour-blind.'

'I see. So I can't really help you after all?'

'Oh, that's not why I wanted you. Though I've always got my eyes open, of course.'

He opened his great mournful eyes very wide to demonstrate. Manning suddenly had a vision of Proctor-Gould as he must have been before he had gone up to John's and bought his first double-breasted blazer in Bodger's the outfitters. He saw him living in his parents' semi-detached house in Anerley or Edgware, filling the box-room with pieces of radio transmitter, writing to pen-friends in Tanganyika and New Zealand, building a home-made sports car out of a motor-cycle engine and beaten biscuit tins.

'No,' he said, 'it's Russians I'm interested in. I got into the business as an undergraduate, really, when I was organizing visits for various Soviet student delegations. It was such a fearfully complicated and long-winded business, dealing with the Soviet authorities in those days – after I'd done a couple of delegations I became the accredited expert, and people began calling me in to arrange delegations and groups and exchanges of every shape and size. I had to start charging a fee to cover the time I spent. The thing I noticed was how much in demand the Russians always were when they were over – everyone wanted them to come to parties, give lectures, appear on television quiz shows, and so on. So I started charging fees to everyone who wanted to borrow them, as well. Pretty soon I had unique contacts with the Soviet authorities, and what was almost a full-time business on my hands.'

'And the Russians are prepared to co-operate in all this?' asked Manning.

'My dear Paul, they fall over themselves to co-operate. The Soviet authorities and I are like *that*.'

He hooked his two index fingers together.

'There have been rough passages, I admit. But there are some bright young men coming to the top in the Ministry of Foreign Affairs these days. I've gradually persuaded them that the best possible advertisement for Russia abroad is not sputniks or coal-cutting machinery, but ordinary common or garden people.'

'Don't they always want you to take only worthy and reliable citizens?'

'They did at first. You should have seen some of the specimens I collected on my first couple of trips! Honestly, Paul,

I practically killed myself trying to work them up into something usable. It was all right as a novelty, but we couldn't possibly have gone on running stuff like that. It was the Yevtushenko affair that changed everything.'

'Was he one of your clients?'

'Alas, no. But the bright young people here began to see that mavericks and rebels like Yevtushenko created not a worse but a better image of Russia in Western eyes. All right, they said, the West refuses to accept that Russia is contented and monolithic. But perhaps it might accept the idea that Russia is a turbulent, intellectually vital country seething with new ideas. For the last couple of years I've been able to get virtually anyone I wanted, provided they were fundamentally loyal, like Yevtushenko. I'm in a position of trust and privilege, of course, and I take care not to abuse it. I might add that the Soviet government recognizes me as having exclusive rights on the whole Soviet market.'

'That's an absolutely staggering achievement,' said Manning, amazed that anyone dressed as Proctor-Gould was could get so far. Proctor-Gould plucked at his ear, and lengthened his long face dismally, to conceal his pleasure at the compliment.

'But I'm told you don't speak Russian,' said Manning.

'Now you've put your finger on it. I don't. I've tried to learn, but I'm afraid I'm just no linguist. Never mastered this comic alphabet they've got. Naturally, most of the people who are going to be presentable as personalities in Britain or the United States speak English. All the same, I think the time has come when we've got to try and get at the real Russia, and that means going far beyond the English-speaking section of society. I work very closely with V.O.K.S., the All-Union Society for Cultural Relations, who provide me with interpreters – and I can always get an Intourist girl from the desk downstairs. But it's not easy to assess the personality of a Russian when it's being filtered through another Russian, with a Russian outlook and Russian preconceptions. What I need, it seems to me, is not a Russian who has learnt English, but an Englishman who knows Russian. I wondered if the job might appeal to you? It would only involve a few hours a week away from your thesis – I can still do all the routine work with a Soviet interpreter. I'll pay you what I'd pay an interpreter in London, two guineas an hour. I'll pay it in sterling, or in Swiss francs, or in roubles at four roubles to the pound. Whichever you prefer.'

Manning held up his spoon, and squinted over it towards the window so that the apostle just covered the domes of the Uspensky Cathedral. He was trying to conceal his pleasure at being offered a job. In the lower depths of the academic world, which he inhabited, jobs were applied and competed for, not offered.

'The vetting was satisfactory, then?' he asked.

'Vetting? Oh, come, come. It was just a few discreet questions.'

'And what did you find out?'

'Just that your Russian is fluent, and that your standing with both the Soviet authorities and the Embassy is reasonably good. That's all I wanted to know.'

'What made you think of me in the first place?'

Proctor-Gould shrugged.

'I heard your name mentioned in London.'

'By whom?'

'I can't really remember. Another old Johnsman, probably, who remembered you were installed over here. The old boy network again, I expect.'

Manning got up and went across to the window. It was a dull, dead day, with a low ceiling of cloud moving slowly over from Smolensk and Mogilev in the west, past Moscow to Sverdlovsk and the unimaginable distances beyond. Tiny figures in grey raincoats and grey fedoras trudged across the great landscape of the square. Here a man in a double-breasted blazer with threads of cotton hanging from the nap could still prosper.

'I take it that this offer is entirely what it seems?' asked Manning suddenly. 'I'm not being recruited for some sort of intelligence work?'

Proctor-Gould turned slowly round towards Manning and gazed at him steadily with his great brown eyes.

'What makes you ask that?'

'I don't know. It was just a thought.'

'I ask you to interpret for me – and the first thought that comes into your head is that it might have something to do with intelligence?'

'Well, one's always hearing of people being approached in some roundabout way.'

Proctor-Gould pulled his ear in silence for a moment or two, gazing sombrely down at the heap of clothes on the floor.

'Let me assure you, Paul,' he said slowly and quietly, 'that this has nothing whatsoever to do with intelligence.'

'I'm sorry. Silly of me to mention it.'

'You accept my word?'

'Yes, of course.'

'And let me ask one thing of you, Paul. Never – ever – refer to intelligence or espionage in the context of our work again, even as a joke.'

'All right.'

'Things get overheard, as you know. They get misunderstood and misreported. And once an idea has been implanted, however preposterous it is, it's almost impossible ever to uproot it again.'

'I'm sorry, Gordon.'

'Don't forget – our work depends on creating confidence.'

From the word 'our' Manning took it that he was considered as engaged. Already he found Proctor-Gould a strangely impressive employer.

8

Manning's life became a round of parties, receptions, conferences, congresses, reunions, exhibitions – all the various bends and corners in life at which a sediment of people might be deposited for inspection. For his purely commercial dealings in balalaikas and Repin prints Proctor-Gould continued to use Soviet interpreters. But there turned out to be a third aspect to his activities which he had not mentioned before, and for which he preferred Manning. He was an export-import agent in goodwill. He had commissions, Manning discovered, from a number of organizations in Britain which wished to maintain or improve their contacts with the Soviet Union. Manning spent hours with him calling on government offices, university departments, and cultural agencies to convey greetings from British counterparts. They shook hands, drank toasts, smiled smiles. Often they delivered gifts, usually books from the stock which Proctor-Gould had referred to as his beads.

'I accept commissions of this sort only from organizations with the right sort of standing,' he explained. 'I help them – their reputation helps me.'

'You do it for nothing?' asking Manning.

'No, no – I charge a modest fee. They're happy to pay it, I can tell you – it costs them far less than it would to send a man of their own over here. And I don't want to boast, but I probably make rather a better job of it than they would themselves. I know from long experience how Russians like these things to be done.'

'You seem to have struck quite a little goldmine,' said Manning.

They were walking down a crowded shopping street as they talked, back to the black Chaika saloon which the government had put at Proctor-Gould's disposal. At Manning's remark Proctor-Gould stopped among the crowds, and fixed Manning with that gaze of curious intensity and levelness which indicated that the subject was so important to him that it took up the whole of his attention.

'Paul,' he said, 'I shouldn't like you to get the wrong impression about my work here. There's nothing cynical about my attitude, I assure you. I happen to believe that there's nothing more important in the world today than the establishment of trust and understanding between Russia and the West. If I can feel that I'm making some small contribution to this end by my professional services, that's my real reward. The money is of secondary importance. I should like you to get that quite clear, Paul.'

Manning believed he was sincere. Proctor-Gould had that patent sincerity directed towards unsubtle objectives which is the strength and hallmark of public men. That was what he was, thought Manning – a public man. He was not interested, as Manning was, in making his contacts with the world around him personal and intimate. Towards his parents, thought Manning, he would make generous formal gestures, as if they were not so much his parents as the emissaries of parents as a social class; towards women, gestures of generalized concupiscence, as if they were not Lucinda or Sally-Anne, but representatives of Lucindahood and Sally-Annity.

Certainly a public life sprang up around them wherever they went in Moscow. On the slightest pretext, at even quite small receptions, Proctor-Gould would make a speech. The phrases which came rolling so steadily and emphatically out on these occasions – 'the cultural treasure-house we share', 'setting our barren suspicions and fears behind us', 'practical steps to increase our mutual confidence' – were not exactly clichés. They were units of the public language. At first their abstraction and generality appalled Manning as he translated them. Yet he could see them have their effect on the audience – the limited effect of public language on a public audience, but an effect nonetheless.

People listened and applauded with genuine respect and interest. An attempt at some more personal form of communication, conceded Manning grudgingly, might have had no effect at all without the framework of a real personal relationship to give it meaning.

It was at an occasion of this nature that Sasha first met Proctor-Gould. A reception was being held for Proctor-Gould in a lecture-room in the History Faculty. It was early evening. The air was full of chalk dust from the blackboard, and the level rays of the setting sun through a western window cut golden swathes across it. Proctor-Gould was speaking when Manning, standing by his side on the dais translating, caught sight of Sasha's wind-lifted tangle of hair glowing like an aureole in one of the bars of light. For a moment he stumbled in his translation. But Sasha was not looking at him. His worried eyes were fixed on Proctor-Gould, screwed up a little as though to peer through the glare of outer appearances into the dark soul within.

After the speeches and presentations were over Manning introduced them. They gazed into each other's sincere brown eyes, crushed each other's hand in a mutually destructive grip, and took to each other immediately. They were evidently pleased by each other's moral seriousness, and after a little preliminary banter, they began to speak with an unashamed earnestness which neither of them would have attempted with Manning, for whose corrupted taste they both assumed the convention of self-deflating humour.

Afterwards the three of them went on to dinner in a restaurant. Manning felt very much the third of the three. He was not needed as an interpreter, since Proctor-Gould and Sasha were speaking English together, and he was lumbered with a large silver-plated model of the university skyscraper with which Proctor-Gould had been presented at the reception. It was he who had to drop back when there was not enough room for three abreast on the pavement, then run a couple of steps to catch up again. It was he who had to interrupt to insist that they decided on a restaurant, as the other two strode towards nowhere, completely absorbed in recalling their mutual childhood passions for stamps, railways, and wireless sets. Manning's relief that his mentor and his employer approved of each other changed to an obscure irritation. It was as if one's parent and one's teacher had taken to each other too readily; a threatening coalition.

In the restaurant the band played 'Ochi Chorniye', Mendelssohn's 'Spring Song', and 'Yes, Sir, That's My Baby', and they had to wait an hour before they were served. Manning sank into a stupor. When he focused his attention on the conversation again, Proctor-Gould was inviting Sasha to come to England as one of his personalities.

'It's kind of you to ask me, Gordon,' Sasha was saying. 'But really, I've no distinction at all in any field of life.'

'I don't want distinguished people, Sasha. I want authentic ones.'

'You mean honest people? Good people?'

'That's not the point. I want *people* people, to quote a phrase I've had occasion to use before.'

The skin at the corners of Sasha's eyes crumpled anxiously.

'People who are in some way representative of the society they live in?'

'No. People who are in some way representative of themselves.'

They gazed at each other. Proctor-Gould was leaning forwards across the empty tablecloth, and there was a slight smile about the corners of his lips. He was enjoying Sasha's mystification, in the way that some men enjoy mystifying women with the esoteric illogicality of masculine concepts of sport and business.

'You see, Sasha,' he explained, 'it's been discovered that certain people have something about them which makes them interesting to their fellow men. Some of them are un-usual people – some of them are very ordinary. Some of them are liked – some of them are disliked. But whatever they do, whether it's in character or out of character, it makes news. People feel they have some sort of relation-ship to them. It's almost as if they felt the personalities were their children. One's interested in whatever one's children do, just because they *are* one's children. Do you see?'

Sasha ran his finger cautiously down the silver sky-scraper, which stood between them on the table like a giant salt-cellar.

'I can understand,' he said, 'that many people, many per-fectly ordinary people, have an interesting story to tell. No one's experience of life is valueless.'

Proctor-Gould glanced at Manning.

'*You* see it,' he said, 'don't you, Paul?'

'I'm not sure,' said Manning. 'I suppose it's something to do with the need to establish one's concept of identity, by concrete examples. Is that right?'

'On the right lines, anyway,' said Proctor-Gould. 'I think it's something that anyone in the West would understand immediately. I'm not preaching, Sasha, but in a sense our interest in personalities is the ultimate expression of our belief in respect for the individual.'

'Of course,' said Sasha, 'we have had the so-called cult of personality here. . . .'

'Our personalities are not in positions of power, Sasha. A respect for pure personality without function – that's what we are aiming at.'

Sasha blinked rapidly.

'In this country,' he said, 'as I believe I once told Paul, a man feels needed. Surely to need someone is the greatest respect you can pay him?'

'To need him, Sasha? To need him for some purpose? For what he can do? For the contribution he can make?'

'Exactly.'

'Isn't that a rather sordid interest, Sasha? To need a man because you can make use of him is to treat him as a tool, as an object. It's exploitation. We say that a man is to be respected not for what he can do for us, but for being the man he is.'

'And you believe this of all men?'

'In theory. In practice we take certain public personalities as symbols of mankind in general, and we attach our respect and interest to these representatives.'

Sasha brooded until the soup arrived.

'Anyway,' said Proctor-Gould, 'the important thing is whether you'd like to come over to England yourself and let me handle you.'

'You really think I'm one of your personalities?'

'I think I could make you one.'

Sasha sighed.

'I wonder,' he said. 'I wonder. I should like to visit England. But at first sight, I must tell you frankly, being a personality in your sense seems to me a little like being a prostitute.'

'A prostitute, Sasha?'

'Offering my person for hire.'

Proctor-Gould's soup spoon had halted half-way to his mouth in astonishment at 'prostitute'. Now he put it carefully back in the soup and fixed Sasha with his special gaze.

'I honestly don't think that's right, Sasha,' he said. 'If it's like anything, it's like an artist offering himself to the public through his art.'

'Would you agree to become a personality yourself, Gordon?'

Proctor-Gould stared at Sasha for some moments, pulling at his ear. Then he suddenly lowered his gaze to the silver university.

'It's a funny thing,' he said, 'but no one's ever asked me that before. I've never thought about it.'

He gazed at the skyscraper for a long time, pulling at his

ear as if he would drag it out by the roots. Sasha and Manning watched him over their soup spoons.

'I think I would,' he said at last. 'I think I would. But I see it's not an entirely straightforward choice.'

'No,' said Sasha, 'it's not. But your ideas are certainly interesting, Gordon. I should like my colleagues in the Faculty to meet you. Perhaps I could arrange a little dinner some time?'

'I should like that, Sasha. Very much.'

'Perhaps towards the end of term? Will you still be here then?'

'Until June at least, Sasha.'

'All right. Meanwhile I shall think about your offer.'

Afterwards, Manning walked back with Proctor-Gould towards his hotel through the cool spring night.

'You won't get him, you know,' said Manning.

'I think I will, Paul.'

'He'll always put his obligations first.'

'But what will he consider his obligations to be? He's an ambitious man, you know.'

'Ambitious?'

'I think so, Paul. I should know – I am myself. That's why we get on so well together. Anyway, we shall get that dinner out of him, if nothing else. It's rather convenient, as a matter of fact – I have a number of messages and presents for people in your Faculty.'

'You never said.'

'No.'

They were outside the Hotel National.

'Will you come up for a late-night Nescafé?' asked Proctor-Gould. Manning shook his head.

'I hadn't thought about Sasha being ambitious,' he said, as they hesitated on the pavement. 'But he's a *good* man, you know.'

'Oh, yes.'

'Are you good, do you believe, Gordon?'

Proctor-Gould shrugged his shoulders.

'It's a question I ask myself,' he said.

9

Manning fell in love, in a way. It was on a suburban train, on the Mozhaisk line, and the girl was sitting in the seat opposite him. She was not, as he had envisaged, sunburnt and wearing a slight cotton dress. She was pale, with very fair hair, and she was wearing a quilted anorak and thick trousers. So was Manning himself, and almost everybody else in the carriage. They were going on a rally or ramble organized by the Faculty Sport Club in the forest outside Moscow under Sasha's leadership.

'Which is it, Paul?' Proctor-Gould had asked Manning when Sasha invited him. 'A rally or a ramble?'

'It depends how far they walk,' Manning had explained gloomily. 'If it's over about ten kilometres it will be rather less of a rally and rather more of a ramble.'

'Ten kilometres? They might go as far as that?'

'Easily. It'll be freezing cold, too, and I should think at this time of year the woods are a sea of mud.'

Proctor-Gould had fingered his ear dubiously. Manning, anxious to avoid the occasion, had urged another drawback.

'They'll sing songs, Gordon.'

Proctor-Gould had at once ceased to finger his ear.

'They'll sing songs, will they, Paul?'

'They'll probably expect you to sing them something, too.'

Proctor-Gould's attitude had changed entirely.

'I rather enjoy a bit of a sing-song, Paul. If the company's congenial. I used to be rather in demand at parties in college. "My Father was the Keeper of the Eddystone Light" –

that kind of thing. Top of the hit parade at John's, setting all false modesty to one side.'

So Manning found himself on the Mozhaisk train, sitting opposite the girl with fair hair. He was not entirely right about the weather. The air temperature was low, but the woods on either side of the train were filled with the most brilliant spring sunlight. Already, however, people had begun to sing. They sang different songs in different parts of the carriage. Manning could hear Sasha's clear, sweet tenor cutting through the confusion of sound, and Proctor-Gould, uttering the curious tuneless booming that comes from a man doing his best to join in a song he has never heard before. Manning hoped he would soon be allowed to get back to his home ground on 'The Eddystone Light'.

The girl with the very fair hair was singing, too. Manning watched her covertly. She had a broad face, with distinct cheekbones and clearly defined eyebrows which were much darker than her hair. She looked as if she might be a post-graduate student or a lecturer, but Manning knew them all, and he had never seen her about the Faculty before. She caught his eyes, and at once stopped singing and lowered her eyelids.

The sight of her disturbed Manning. It threatened him with the necessity for making decisions and taking initiatives. The long and involved processes of human courtship might be about to start. If he made a move ... If she responded at all ... He hedged himself about with conditions and concessions. Already he could see how stupid the things would be that he would tell her to try and impress her. Already he could feel the terrible uncertainty he would go through about whether to take her hand, whether to put his arm round her and kiss her. As if it was already past history he knew exactly what he would feel on the days when she said she couldn't see him, and how irritatingly plain she would look as she came towards him along the street. He shifted uneasily in his seat at the thought of it.

This really was the worst moment in the whole awful business of courtship, the moment before it started. If indeed it did start.

He caught her eye again. They both quickly looked away. He turned his head slowly from the view out of the left-hand window to the view out of the right-hand one, so that he could let his eyes travel over her face in passing. Almost immediately he had to turn his head back from right to left to take another look at her. Once more their eyes met, and hastily parted again. He stared out of the window at the telegraph poles going by, knowing his face was loaded with a meaningless frown. What a stupid business! Did he really have to go ahead with it? He could have groaned aloud, he felt such a fool. And yet, beneath all the confusion and indecision, the current of sweet excitement ran on. It was like a brook one could hear rippling unseen beneath tangled undergrowth.

They all got off the train at a small country station surrounded by open fields, and in the confusion of identical anoraks Manning lost sight of the girl. On the horizon to the north the fields were bounded by the dark green line of the forest. Straggling like a column of deserters they set off towards it along a muddy farm track, skirting the long puddles of water in the ruts. From a group of farm buildings in the distance came the sound of loudspeakers playing a march, fading and returning in the cool breaths of wind. Gradually the snatches of music grew fainter and ceased. The great stillness of the country settled over them.

In the way that drinkers find themselves, to their surprise, in bars, Manning found himself walking beside the girl with the fair hair.

'Hallo again,' he said smoothly.

'Hallo,' said the girl, glancing at him, and then dropping her eyes.

They walked along in silence; Manning couldn't think of anything else to say. People tried to get the singing going again, but it quickly died away. They were all too put out, in spite of themselves, by the change from effortless and tidy locomotion to propelling themselves by their own efforts along the uneven and slippery track.

The girl stopped to pick up a snail shell. Manning saw that she was already holding a number of objects – a pearl-grey wing feather, a pebble, a chalk-white segment from some animal's backbone.

'I like your collection,' he said.

'Do you?'

'Yes, I do.'

'Oh.'

'Perhaps I could help you find some more things?'

'Perhaps you could.'

Manning felt pleased with himself. He had made plenty of worse opening moves than that. An assured and worldly note had been struck, he felt.

'You just look at the ground, do you?' he asked.

'Yes.'

'As you go along?'

'That's right.'

Manning gazed seriously at the ground, looking for topics of conversation. Almost without their noticing it, the outskirts of the forest closed in around them.

'Do you like rambles?' asked Manning.

'Quite.'

'What about rallies?'

'Yes.'

'Which do you prefer?'

'I'm not sure,' she said, and gave a small laugh.

They were getting on quite well, thought Manning. A very uncomplicated, idyllic relationship was being established.

'A crow,' he said, pointing at one.

'Yes?' she said expectantly.

'I said, a crow.'

'What about the crow?'

'I was just remarking that it was a crow.'

She gave another little laugh.

'I see,' she said.

Inside the forest the country was broken, and no two acres of it were alike. At one moment they would be walking over dry pine needles, across long slopes that revealed nothing but ranks of dark conifer trunks in every direction. At the next they would be in birch country, following water-logged clay tracks which twisted down through sudden pockets of open valley filled with sunshine. Speckled patches of snow lit the shadows and northern slopes. People got their second wind, and began to sing again.

'I've never seen you around the Faculty,' said Manning.

'No?'

'No.'

They had been walking for about an hour when pungent woodsmoke drifted towards them through the trees, and the sound of resinous timber crackling and spitting in the fire. They came to a clearing hazy with the smoke. There were shouts of recognition – it was the advance party, roasting potatoes and boiling millet porridge.

They sat down and ate. The black from the potatoes got over their faces, and the millet porridge tasted of nothing. Presently they sang. Manning watched the girl as she took the time from Sasha. He was definitely getting off with her – he really was doing very well. An agreeable feeling of confidence and experience seized him.

'Now,' said Sasha, 'let's have a song from our two English friends.'

Proctor-Gould looked at Manning. Manning shook his head firmly.

'In that case,' said Proctor-Gould, getting to his feet and addressing the company, 'I shall have to ask for your forbearance and offer my humble services as a soloist. With your kind permission I should like to sing you a rather light-hearted little song entitled, "My Father Was the Keeper of the Eddystone Light".'

He sang. It was considerably worse than Manning had expected. Proctor-Gould hunted about for each note uncertainly, and did not often find it. Manning looked round at the girl and smiled. She gazed at Proctor-Gould seriously, no doubt baffled by the strange modes of English song.

'Incidentally,' whispered Manning, leaning close to her ear, 'my name is Paul.'

'Oh,' she said. 'I'm glad.'

'You're Glad?'

'Yes.'

Manning tried the name over to himself. *Rada* – Glad. He had never heard of anyone called Rada before.

'It suits you,' he whispered.

'What?'

'Your name – Glad. It's beautiful.'

She stared at him. Then she whispered:

'Do you know what I think, Paul?'

'No?'

'I think you're a buffoon.'

Proctor-Gould reached the end of his song, and there was a certain amount of polite, baffled clapping. The girl got up and walked away to the other side of the clearing.

'Thank you, thank you,' said Proctor-Gould. 'Your very generous response encourages me to go on and sing you another very old favourite in England, "Green Grow the Rushes Oh".'

A stupid-looking man next to Manning who had been trying for some time to open a bottle of fizzy fruit-juice by thumping it up and down against the ground at last succeeded. The cap exploded off the bottle, and contents rose into the air like a geyser, then fell as a fine, sticky rain over Manning.

'"I'll sing you one-oh",' sang Proctor-Gould. 'No, no, I'll start again. Might as well begin on the right note. "I'll

sing you –" No. "I'll –" Hm. "I'll –" H'hgm. "I'll sing you
one-oh ..."'

Manning slipped away into the woods out of earshot.
The whole expedition was intolerable.

10

Manning relieved himself gloomily in a quiet corner of the
forest. As he finished, something struck him sharply on the
shoulder. It was a piece of dead wood. He looked round.
About twenty feet away stood the girl with fair hair. She
was looking round a birch tree at him, resting her head
against the trunk, and biting at a twig she had bent down
from the branch above her so that she showed her teeth.
She looked like a shot out of a silent film.

'My name's Raya,' she said, taking the twig out of her
mouth. 'If you're interested.'

'Oh,' said Manning, rubbing his shoulder, and confused
to find that she had been watching him.

'Why didn't you ask me what my name actually was?'

'You didn't seem very keen to talk.'

'Oh,' said Raya. She bit thoughtfully at the birch twig.
'I thought I was being flirtatious.'

'I see. I didn't realize.'

'Perhaps I didn't do it right.'

'Oh – yes, yes.'

'When I went away I thought you'd follow me.'

'I didn't grasp that at all, I'm afraid.'

She chewed the twig for some moments.

'I obviously wasn't going about it the right way,' she
said. 'Do you want to know what my job is?'

'All right. What is it?'

'I teach Diamat.'

'Diamat? Dialectical materialism?'

'Why do you say it in that tone of voice?'

'Well, I don't know – you don't look much like a teacher of dialectical materialism.'

'Oh? What do teachers of dialectical materialism look like, in your experience?'

'Well, not *blonde*, somehow.'

Raya pulled a handful of her hair forward and squinted at it.

'It's not really blonde,' she said. 'I bleached it. Do you like it?'

'Very much.'

'You wouldn't prefer to see it red, or black?'

'Certainly not.'

Raya reflected.

'I'm being flirtatious now,' she said. 'Do you realize? There's a terrible coyness about the conversation that you couldn't account for in any other way. Let's go for a walk.'

They walked slowly through the woods, stepping over fallen branches and skirting patches of brambles.

'You left your friend to sing on his own,' said Raya.

'You left your friends to listen on their own.'

'My friends?'

'Your colleagues in the Faculty.'

'Not my colleagues – not my Faculty. I teach in the Journalism Faculty.'

'What on earth are you doing on the Admin-Uprav outing, then?'

'That's not a very hospitable attitude.'

'I meant, did someone bring you?'

'I brought myself.'

'Brought yourself?'

'Why not? The railways are a public utility. The forest belongs to the state.'

Manning felt curiously irritated by her self-confidence.

'The millet porridge belonged to Admin-Uprav,' he said.

'I admit,' said Raya, 'I obtained a helping of millet porridge by false pretences.'

They walked along in silence, Raya flicking at the trees with her birch twig.

'But why did you particularly want to come on the Admin-Uprav expedition, then?'

'Can't you guess?'

'No.'

Raya danced two steps, held out her hand in front of her, and kicked it, like a ballet-dancer.

'No idea?' she said.

'Not the slightest.'

'Shall I give you a clue?'

'All right.'

She leaned over and kissed him on the ear.

He put his hand up to the ear, as if it had been struck. What curious organisms human beings were, he reflected. How odd and unfamiliar were the relations between them, like the interactions of half-understood particles beneath the microscope.

'Was that the clue?' he asked. His own voice seemed no less strange to him that Raya's behaviour.

'The clue? Comrade Interpreter, it was practically the *solution*.'

He should no doubt kiss her back. He turned towards her, but she stepped away from him. He lunged at her – she leapt out of reach. He chased her up the path – she doubled back round a tree, and in the ensuing jinking and bobbing to left and to right they cracked their heads together painfully.

'Oh God!' she cried, as they both rubbed their skulls. 'What a pastoral idyll!'

They started to walk along the path again. He took her hand, but after a little while she withdrew it.

'Well,' he said.

'Everyone in Moscow seems to be talking about your

friend Proctor-Gould,' she said. 'I just wanted to see what sort of people you were.'

'Why didn't you kiss Proctor-Gould's ear?'

'I can't speak English.'

'You don't have to speak to kiss someone's ear.'

'There seems to be a terrible lot of explanation to go through before the appropriate moment arrives.'

'I could interpret.'

Raya glanced at Manning ironically.

'Thanks,' she said. 'A love affair through an interpreter. That's a very cultured prospect.'

They came to a clearing covered with brambles and rank grass. Among the vegetation the half-obliterated remains of trenches and banks were just visible.

'Zhukov made his stand before Moscow in the forest here,' said Raya. 'It's an odd place to come for picnics, really.'

She wandered moodily about the clearing, kicking at the grass, then bent down and picked something up. It was an old steel helmet, thick with rust, a jagged hole in the side.

'You still find these all over the woods,' she said. 'I'm not even sure whether it's Russian or German.'

She turned it slowly over and over in her hands, crumbling more of the rusty metal off. Then she hurled it away, and brushed the rust off her hands. The helmet hit a tree, bounced off in a shower of rust, and fell into a bramble bush, where it perched on a branch, bobbing up and down like some great brown bird alighting. Raya seemed to be abashed by the ridiculousness of it, and picked it out of the bush. They sat down side by side on a fallen tree trunk, sodden, like everything else, with the stored wetness of winter. Raya turned the helmet over in her hands again, feeling its texture curiously.

'Poor old helmet,' she said. 'Manufactured and issued and worn and punctured and lost and rusted by the forces of historical necessity. Found and touched and lost again by Raissa P. Metelius, lecturer.'

She jumped up restlessly, dropping the helmet, and pulled Manning to his feet.

'Come on!' she said.

She was excited and nervous. Manning put his arms round her and kissed her mouth, but after a few seconds she broke away and ran off into the trees. Now she was laughing. He caught up with her and kissed her again. They fell into the wet grass together. Laughing and laughing, Raya sat up and stuffed handfuls of dead leaves into his mouth.

He was sitting up and spitting out the leaves when an unhappy thought occurred to him. It was too good to be true. That was what was wrong with it. She had joined the expedition uninvited – sat opposite him in the train – followed him into the forest – kissed him. The whole thing was being organized not by him but by her. Wasn't it all somewhat reminiscent of those cases one heard about, where foreigners in Russia were compromised, and then blackmailed into working for Soviet intelligence? The idea was ridiculous. All the same ... He stopped where he was, on one knee, a leaf still hanging on his chin. It was a horribly anaphrodisiac thought.

'What is it?' asked Raya, alarmed by the expression on his face. She ran back and knelt beside him.

'Nothing,' said Manning. 'I was just wondering ...'

'Wondering what?'

'If all this wasn't just some sort of trick.'

'How do you mean, a trick?'

'You know, to compromise me. Or Proctor-Gould. The way it's done sometimes. So the authorities can have some kind of lever against us.'

She stared at him, her hand on his arm, as if he was telling her he had some sort of pain. Then she began to smile.

'You think I might be working for the K.G.B.?'

'It was just a sudden thought.'

Raya jumped up and clapped her hands.

'It was a good thought,' she said. 'From the historical-dialectical point of view it was a fruitful and positive thought.'

'It's happened, Raya.'

'Certainly. And will again. I have photographers concealed behind the trees waiting to snap the slightest lewd gesture.'

'People have been photographed, Raya.'

Suddenly she swung round and shouted across to a thicket of birches some twenty yards away. 'Quick, Misha – *now*! While his trousers are still undone!'

Manning's hand flashed down to his trousers. They were done up. Raya started to laugh, and he began to laugh too. They sat on the ground looking at one another and laughing. She pushed him down, and seized his ears, and banged his head gently up and down on the dead leaves, still laughing helplessly.

II

They walked soberly through the woods, holding hands.

'All the same,' said Manning. 'I don't know, do I?'

'No, you don't.'

'Are you?'

'What's the good of my answering? It would be meaningless.'

'All the same.'

'You want a meaningless answer?'

'It's better than none '

'All right, then. I *am* leading you into a trap.'

'Don't joke, Raya.'

'You see?'

'I know perfectly well you're not.'

'All right – I'm not.'

They walked in silence, looking at the ground.

'You wouldn't think we'd only set eyes on one another about four hours ago,' said Manning.

'Judging by some of the things that have been said, I'm astonished it's more than four minutes.'

'You see my point, though.'

'Oh, yes.'

They became silent again.

'Would you *mind* if people knew you'd held my hand in the woods?' asked Raya.

'Of course not.'

'Well, then.'

'But we might do more than just hold hands.'

'Might we?'

'Well, mightn't we?'

They stopped and looked at each other gravely. Then Raya lowered her eyes and began to play with the button on his jacket.

'*Am* I acting in good faith?' she asked quietly.

He did not reply.

'Go on,' she insisted, still quietly, running her hands over the fabric of his jacket, as she had over the helmet. 'Tell me what you think. Am I?'

'I don't know.'

'To hell with you, then!' she said, suddenly angry, and pushed him away. He stepped back to keep his balance, caught his heel against the root of a tree, and fell full length into a bramble patch, discarded like the rusty helmet. He shouted with surprise, and with pain, as the thorns scratched his hands and his ears. He thrashed wildly about, trying to find a thornless patch to lever himself up from. When he looked up he saw that Raya was leaning against a tree silently weeping – no, silently laughing, reduced to the helpless silence of laughter. He struggled to his feet and rushed at her in a fury, though he was unclear exactly what he intended to do. But she ran away, shouting with laughter, dodging among the trees, always keeping just ahead of him.

In the end she leapt into the fork of a birch and climbed swiftly out of reach. He leaned against the trunk and looked up at her, panting too hard to reproach her. She squatted on her branch and gazed down at him, panting too hard to laugh at him. She was just a child, thought Manning, a silly, teasing child. Suddenly he did not think he understood her at all, and he seized the tree and shook it with all his might, trying to shake her down like an apple.

'That's right,' she cried. 'Break the tree down. Cause damage to plant life in the state forest.'

Eventually she jumped down, kissed his scratches better, put her arm in his, and walked on through the forest with him. They walked with their eyes on the ground six feet in front of them, the way people do, as if for ever contemplating the measure of earth they must one day become.

Their path joined a track, and over the track, where it entered the mouth of a little valley, there was an arch formed of two bare birch trunks and a roughly painted sign between them which said: 'Rest and Holiday Centre "Forest Lake"'.

They followed the track down to the lake – a large pond, really, trapped in the valley bottom. The water sparkled in the sun. On the shore was a settlement of shabby wooden cabins, all shuttered and deserted, with sky-blue paintwork which was blistered and peeling. Raya and Manning wandered among the cabins, moved by such silence and stillness in a place where human beings had lived. They squatted on the little wooden landing stage and peered into the dark water. A fish glided, flicked, and was gone.

In that sheltered corner of the woods it was warm. They stretched out on the boards and lay quietly with their faces to the sun. After a little while Raya lifted her head and looked about her sleepily, like a cat.

'Do you like swimming?' she asked.

'Not in water as cold as this.'

'We could swim across the lake and back, as fast as porpoises.'

'We'd freeze, Raya.'

'No, we shouldn't. We'd jump out, and rub each other dry, and lie here in the sun on the landing stage, and stroke each other till we were warm.'

They looked at each other softly, taunting each other with the uncertainty of what could or could not happen.

There was a cry from the other side of the lake. They turned round. It was Sasha. He waved to them anxiously.

'I suppose they've been looking for us,' said Manning. 'I'd forgotten all about them.'

'I suppose I had, too,' said Raya. She gazed sadly across the water at Sasha, and waved a small wave back at him. He turned and began to hurry round the lake towards them, his shock of dark, thin hair sweeping anxiously, responsibly back in the wind of his passage.

12

Walking in the twilight with Katerina. Somewhere. Along some narrow busy street lined with decrepit old apartment houses. As they passed each entry the excited screaming of the children playing in the darkened courtyard within for a moment joined the roar of the buses and lorries stinking by at Manning's elbow. Along the narrow pavement people were streaming home from work, tired, looking down, their faces in shadow. Constantly they passed between Manning and Katya, forcing him to stop or to step off the kerb, and then run a step to catch up.

Manning was surprised that there were still streets left in Moscow that he did not know. He felt as if he and Katya had walked down every single one of them – a hundred miles of asphalt, of concrete slabs, of beaten earth, of packed, trodden snow. He wondered how many of the people they passed were walking for the same reason as themselves, that the public street was the only private place to talk. All over Moscow the streets must have been alive with communal intimacy. Two by two the talkers walked, passing, overtaking, and intersecting, as if the city were some vast, complex cloister. Visions of a new society were exchanged, love affairs were pursued and broken off, arrangements to circumvent the law and defraud the state were entered into. As he ran along the gutter to catch up with Katya, Manning laughed out loud at the ridiculous discomfort of their accommodation. Katya, hurrying along in her winter overcoat, gave him one of her quick, mistrustful glances. She said something, but it was drowned in the sudden high coloratura of a bus with bad brakes.

'I said,' she repeated, 'I'm happy for your happiness.'

'I was just laughing at us.'

'Oh. Is Raya beautiful?'

Manning considered. Would being beautiful count for or against Raya in Katya's eyes? He was frightened of her judgement. He could see Raya through Katya's eyes, and she became insignificant – as insignificant as Katya herself would certainly seem to Raya.

'I think perhaps she is,' he said cautiously.

'Would *I* think she was?'

'You might.'

'I wonder.'

'I'm surprised you're interested.'

'I like to think of a woman being beautiful, since I'm not myself. I like to think that you should find a beautiful woman.'

'Really?'

'I'm not jealous, Paul. You wouldn't like me to be, would you? I thought I might feel jealous of Raya when you first began to describe her. Or rather, not of her, but of your feeling for her. It's easy to be jealous of love, even when it's

58

experienced by someone with whom one's not in love oneself. You are a little jealous of my love of God. It makes
you wonder whether you have that same capacity yourself.
You think you don't want to love God or be loved by Him,
but you cannot help wondering whether you could if you
did. Was Sasha jealous?'

'Sasha? How could he be? You don't think he's in love
with Raya?'

'I meant jealous of her hold on you.'

'You think he's in love with *me*?'

'He's like a conscientious father with a delinquent son.
He doesn't much like you. But he has an obsessiveness about
you which might count as a sort of love.'

'Perhaps he *was* a bit jealous.'

'He became very polite and withdrawn and solicitous?'

'Yes. When he found us by the lake he said they'd been
looking for us for over an hour. I hadn't realized we'd been
gone more than ten minutes. He'd wanted to go to the
police. I felt like a badly behaved child, as usual.'

'Did Raya?'

'No. She was amused. She started to tease Sasha. When
we got on the train to come home, for example she threw
the rucksack at the rack so that it just missed and fell back
on Sasha's head. It probably sounds a bit silly. But it was
the way she did it. . .'

'I see.'

'And she kept apologizing. "I'm dreadfully sorry," she
said. "I underfulfilled my plan, Alexander Timofeyich".'

'Timofeyich? Is that really Sasha's patronymic?'

'No.'

'Were you amused?'

'Well, I was. It may not sound very funny as I tell it, but
at the time . . .'

'Yes, I see that. Poor Sasha.'

'Poor Sasha? But I thought you disapproved of him,
Katya?'

'Oh, Paul! We always have this conversation; I explain to you every time. Sasha's good – how could I not approve of him? In fact I admire him. It's just that I'm *opposed* to him, because he is on the side of the strong, and I'm on the side of the weak.'

'I know. I know. But you're able to feel sorry for him?'

'It's terrible when good people are teased by bad people.'

Manning danced with a burly man in a shabby blue overcoat, trying to pass to left and to right, then ran to catch up with Katya, who had not stopped or slowed down.

'Raya isn't bad . . .' he began.

'I didn't mean that,' she interrupted. 'At least, I didn't mean to mean it.'

'You think it.'

'I have no opinion. I have excised my opinion.'

After a little while she asked:

'Is Raya good, then, Paul?'

'I think so, Katya.'

'When you asked yourself, as you must have done, whether she had attached herself to you for sincere motives or because she was told to, what answer did you find?'

'Well, I've no proof either way. How could I have?'

'You've no proof about my motives, either. But you're sure of me.'

'Oh, Katya, with you the question doesn't arise.'

'But it does with her?'

'I think I'm satisfied.'

'It's a difference between us.'

'Oh, yes.'

Katya was silent.

'Is she perhaps good in the way that Sasha is good?' she asked finally.

'Katya!' cried Manning. 'You're obsessed with goodness!'

'No, no – I'm obsessed with God, of whom goodness is the physical radiance. When I ask if Raya is good, I mean, is she God-filled, in the way that Sasha is God-filled?'

'Sasha God-filled? How can he be? He's an atheist.'

'Sasha's opinions about himself are irrelevant.'

'But, Katya, I don't understand at all! You think that Sasha is strong. But you also think that God is on the side of the weak!'

'Oh, Paul! God doesn't take sides! It's I who take sides.'

'Against Sasha? Against God within him?'

Katya became very agitated. She began to walk more quickly, so that Manning had difficulty in keeping up. She flushed, and pressed her fingers to her lips. Manning wondered if she was going to cry.

'I don't know where my thoughts lead,' she said at last. 'Must I turn my hand against God? But my hand *is* God! God against God! What confusion! What problems we've been set!'

13

Manning took Raya to the theatre, to the cinema, to the ballet, and wherever they went people turned to look at her.

He had to get the tickets for these occasions from the foreign students' allotment, through Sasha. Sasha produced them reluctantly; he could not conceal his uneasiness that the relationship was continuing. Under the stained portrait of Lenin in his office he had one of his 'serious talks' with Manning about the need for getting ahead with his thesis, particularly since he had already chosen to give up time to interpreting for Proctor-Gould. He insisted on taking them both out to dinner one evening, in the way that a possessive mother insists on inviting her son's unsuitable girl friend home, in the hope that she will not survive the light of day. It was a tiring occasion. Whenever Raya spoke, Sasha frowned anxiously, strained by his determination to be scrupulously fair to her. But instead of being subdued by it, she was amused. Manning saw her mouth straightening at the corners with the effort of not smiling.

'What's your favourite dish, Raya?' asked Sasha politely, as they discussed the merits of the food in front of them.

'Young men, Sasha,' said Raya, her eyes modestly downcast, 'served by the half-dozen with flowers and chocolates.'

Sasha did not invite them again.

Proctor-Gould, as well, knew about the affair. Manning rapidly spent all the money he had earned from interpreting, and had to ask him for twenty roubles on account. Proctor-Gould disapproved, too.

'None of my business, I know, Paul,' he said, 'but I shouldn't get too serious about Raya, if I were you. I've known this sort of thing happen before. A chap over here, in your position, starts some sort of monkey business with one of these Russian girls, and it all ends up in the most unholy mess – usually with the man in question being deported. Then there's always the possibility that you might find yourself being blackmailed. Have you ever thought of that?'

'Yes.'

'Well, take my tip, Paul – the game's not worth the candle. A little light banter over the dinner-table, yes. Anything more – definitely no. I've made myself a rule, Paul – and I may say I've observed it scrupulously – never to get myself emotionally involved over here, however delightful the young lady may be.'

And he invited them both to the opera.

'You won't tease him, will you, Raya?' pleaded Manning, who foresaw another evening like the one with Sasha. 'He takes himself very seriously. Just listen to what he says and agree with it.'

'All right,' said Raya.

The opera was *Khovanshchina*. From time to time during the acts Manning turned to watch Proctor-Gould in the

darkness. He was, he saw, trying to find some way of prop-
ping his head; the lids were coming down over his eyes.
But between the acts, as the three of them paced about the
buffet and the corridors, he was soulful and moved.

'Wonderful singing!' he said, shaking his head solemnly.
'Wonderful singing!'

Manning translated this to Raya.

'Tell Gordon I'm very pleased to hear him say that,' she
replied, 'because it's exactly what I thought.'

Manning translated. Proctor-Gould stroked his ear, lugubriously pleased.

'Ask Gordon,' said Raya, 'if he didn't think the soprano
was a little harsh in the upper registers.'

'Tell Raya that I did,' replied Proctor-Gould. 'Just a shade,
in my opinion.'

'Tell Gordon,' said Raya, 'that I think that's a most perceptive judgement.'

Proctor-Gould lengthened his face judicially when he
heard this.

'Tell Gordon,' said Raya, 'that it's very agreeable to have
one's intuitive feelings confirmed by a connoisseur.'

'Oh, hardly a connoisseur, I'm afraid,' said Proctor-Gould.
'Just someone who enjoys a little fine singing when the
occasion arises.'

'Tell Gordon he understands fine singing because he sings
himself.'

In the next interval Proctor-Gould insisted on standing
them a bottle of champagne in the buffet. He toasted Raya.
Raya toasted Proctor-Gould. Proctor-Gould toasted Manning
and Raya jointly. They all became a little dizzy.

'I must say, Paul,' said Proctor-Gould to Manning in a
low voice, 'I congratulate you on your lady-friend.'

'I thought you were rather against the whole idea?' said
Manning.

'Oh, in *principle*, Paul, yes.'

'You haven't changed your mind about the principle?'

'No, no. I'm still opposed to the principle of the thing.'

After the opera they strolled about the streets, pleased with each other and unwilling to break the evening up. The night was mild; summer was undoubtedly drawing on. It was, thought Manning, in the evenings that the approach of summer first showed itself. On the night that the amputated man had laughed at him outside Komsomolskaya Metro there had been that sense of desolation in the air which makes itself felt as the light fades at the end of even the most brilliant winter day. But tonight there was no tinge of sadness or loneliness at all. Already you could feel the first suggestion of the excitement and anticipation that comes down with the twilight in early summer.

The mood seemed to have affected Raya.

'You know what everyone's talking about in Moscow?' she asked. 'It's the local hooliganism. You can't possibly leave without taking part in it. Come on, let's all hold hands. That's uncultured for a start.'

She took their hands. She made them run across the road at a place where pedestrians were not allowed to cross. She spat on the pavement – they had a spitting competition, which she won. She got Proctor-Gould to sing the 'Internationale'. They trotted, hands still linked, through a grocery store on Gorky Street, barging against the late-night shoppers. Proctor-Gould caught Manning's eye. He pulled his ear with his free hand and giggled.

'It's good for the system to behave childishly sometimes, Paul,' he said.

She trotted them all the way down to the Nikita Gates, then pulled them up short, and pointed at a bed of tulips behind a low railing in the public gardens.

'That would be *real* hooliganism,' she said, 'to steal a municipal tulip.'

Manning hesitated.

'I think that might be going a bit far, honestly, Raya . . .' he began dubiously.

'What does she want?' panted Proctor-Gould.

'A tulip.'

Proctor-Gould pulled his ear once, then trotted across to the railing, clambered awkwardly over, and snapped one off. Manning watched him as he trotted back with the flower. He had never noticed before that Proctor-Gould's body was long and his legs were short – when he ran his bottom seemed to be almost resting on the ground. Manning wondered if he would look impressive placed on a pedestal in Gorky Street opposite the Statue of Yuri Long-Arm, the founder of Moscow, labelled as Gordon Long-Bottom, the finder of people.

Proctor-Gould presented Raya with the flower, then suddenly seized her hand and kissed it.

'Oh, Gordon!' said Raya, laughing. 'Oh, Gordon!'

She held the tulip up, and looked at it carefully. Then she put it in her mouth and ate it, crunching it up like raw cabbage.

'In this health-giving and nutritious way, Gordon,' she said, 'I conceal the evidence of your crime against the state.'

14

Manning could not help being pleased that Raya had made such an impression on Proctor-Gould. Proctor-Gould invited them both out to dinner again. Throughout the meal he behaved with a sort of archaic vulgar gallantry. He proposed toasts to Raya's bright eyes, and to the ladies, God bless them. He asked Manning to ask Raya if there were any more at home like her. He leant forward as he waited for Manning to translate, so that his head got down near the tablecloth, and he had to look up at her with his great brown eyes as if he were an adoring dog looking over the edge of the table. Manning felt that Proctor-Gould's compliments were indirectly compliments to himself. He translated them fully, wherever possible improving upon them and making them more fantastic in the Russian. Raya watched Proctor-Gould gravely as he spoke, and continued to watch him gravely as Manning translated. Sometimes she would laugh, and Proctor-Gould would at once pull his ear and giggle. He had undoubtedly fallen for her. Manning found it amusing to watch.

It was while they were waiting, interminably, for the last course to arrive that a note of discord was struck.

'Tell Raya,' said Proctor-Gould, 'that she has the most beautiful natural blonde hair I've ever seen.'

Manning told her, raising one eyebrow to show that he appreciated the unconscious irony of the compliment. But Raya replied:

'Tell Gordon I have Finnish blood.'

'What's this about Finnish blood?' said Manning. 'I thought it was bleach?'

Raya frowned.

'You think my hair's *bleached*?'

'That's what you told me.'

'Look at it with your own eyes! Do you seriously believe that's not natural blonde hair?'

'What's the argument,' demanded Proctor-Gould.

'Oh, nothing,' said Manning.

'Tell him,' said Raya.

'She says her hair's fair because she has Finnish blood. But she told me the other day that it was because she bleached it.'

'Ask Gordon what he thinks,' insisted Raya. She pulled a handful of hair forward for him to feel. He rubbed it between finger and thumb, smiling foolishly, and touched it against his lips.

'Of course it's natural,' he said. 'It's the most beautiful honey blonde hair I've ever seen. I expect she was teasing you the other day, Paul. She's a terrible tease, you know.'

'What did he say?' demanded Raya, when Manning hesitated.

'He doesn't know what he's talking about.'

'Translate it, all the same,' she ordered. He did so.

'Gordon is a good judge of women,' she said. 'He knows how to appreciate them, and how to deal with them. Tell him so.'

'She says you know how to suck up to people,' Manning told Proctor-Gould sourly. He felt irritated at being teased in front of Proctor-Gould. No doubt Raya was intelligent enough to see that Proctor-Gould was one of those men who were attracted to a woman only when she was already attached to someone else. No doubt she was making use of him merely as a fulcrum against which to lever Manning. All the same ... All the same, the world no longer seemed quite as simple as it had on that day in the forest, when he had lain beside the lake with Raya in the still sunshine. The thought was a sad one.

'Tell Raya,' said Proctor-Gould, 'that I should like her to consider coming to England as one of my clients.'

Manning stared at him.

'This is rather sudden, isn't it?' he said. 'Are you sure it's a serious proposition?'

Proctor-Gould shook his head reproachfully.

'Paul,' he said, 'you're supposed to interpret what I say, you know, not argue about it.'

'I'm not on duty now, Gordon.'

'I thought you were, Paul.'

'Surely this is a social occasion, not a business one.'

'In my profession all occasions are business ones. In any case, I'm paying you, Paul.'

'Don't be silly, Gordon.'

'I paid you for the evening we went to the opera.'

'Will you please tell me what's going on?' Raya asked Manning.

'Anyway, Gordon,' said Manning, 'I think you'd have to admit that this case is a little different.'

'In what way?'

'Well, frankly, this seems to be more like a personal interest than a professional one.'

'Paul, you don't *own* Raya, you know.'

'Translation!' cried Raya.

'I think,' said Manning, 'it's reasonable for me to ask on her behalf exactly what you have in mind.'

'Anyway, you put it to her.'

'I mean, she's very different to the other clients you've lined up, isn't she?'

'Translation!' shouted Raya, banging her hand on the table, so that other people in the restaurant looked round and stared at them.

'They're all different, Paul.'

'But she's a young girl.'

'You make it sound as if she were under the age of consent.'

'Well, she's a personal friend. I'm not sure that I like the idea of her parading herself about in front of the public.'

'*Translation!*'

Reluctantly, Manning told her what Proctor-Gould was proposing. She accepted at once with a brief nod – so brief that the other two did not immediately take it in.

'How does she feel about it?' asked Proctor-Gould. 'Tell her I think her wonderful directness and charm will communicate remarkably well, even though she doesn't know English.'

'He thinks your lack of English would make it rather difficult,' translated Manning. 'Anyway, there's no need to decide now. Think about it over the next couple of weeks and ask him to explain it to you in detail some time.'

'I've said yes already,' replied Raya. 'I understand the project perfectly well.'

'What does she say?'

'She seems to be mildly interested.'

'*Yes, please,*' said Raya to Proctor-Gould, in English. '*Yes, yes, yes, yes, yes, yes, please.*'

Proctor-Gould began to grin, and then to tug at his ear as if to pull some string which would stop him grinning. He gave Raya his Russian business card, with his name printed on it in Cyrillic characters. She took a dozen playing-cards out of her pocket, selected one of them, the ten of diamonds, and wrote her name and the address of the Journalism Faculty among the diamonds. She had never given her private address to Manning, either.

'What were you arguing about a moment or two back?' she asked Manning.

'If you want to know,' he replied sourly, 'I was just trying to make sure that Proctor-Gould intended the invitation seriously, and wasn't just trying to take advantage of you.'

She laughed, and kissed him.

'That was kind of you,' she said. 'My knight! My own trade union representative!'

15

They walked to the Hotel National, the three of them, arm in arm, in silence.

'Well,' said Manning, when they reached the entrance. 'We'll be saying good night, Gordon. I'll see Raya to the bus.'

'Good night, then,' said Proctor-Gould, giving Raya a peck on the cheek and detaching his arm from hers. 'I'm sorry we had words, Paul.'

'It was my fault. I was behaving ridiculously.'

'We were both a little hasty.'

'Yes.'

'Well, good night, then.'

'Good night.'

Manning and Raya turned to go.

'You won't step up to my place for a late-night Nescafé?' said Proctor-Gould, hesitating.

'I don't think we will, thanks, Gordon. Good night.'

Proctor-Gould made gestures to Raya of lifting a cup and drinking, raising his eyebrows interrogatively.

'What's he saying?' Raya asked Manning.

'Oh, he's just asking us if we'd like to have a cup of coffee with him. I said we wouldn't.'

'Oh, but I *would*,' said Raya. She turned to Proctor-Gould. '*Yes, please*,' she said in English. 'Kofye – *yes, please*!'

'Oh, for heaven's sake, Raya! It's far too late.'

'Then you go home, Mr. Interpreter. But for me – *yes, please, yes, please, yes, please.*'

They rode up in the lift, Manning angry, Raya impassive, Proctor-Gould with a soulful light in his capacious eyes which Manning recognized as a sign that he was pleased with himself. Manning did not believe that the floor-clerk would allow Proctor-Gould to take guests to his room at this time of night. But when they got out of the lift and came face to face with the old woman behind the shaded light at the desk Proctor-Gould nodded familiarly to her, and she nodded amiably back.

Raya was intrigued and repelled by the room. While Proctor-Gould fetched the boiling water, she walked about, picking up heaps of socks and underwear from the floor, letting them trickle back through her fingers, then shivering, as if the cold loneliness of Proctor-Gould's way of life struck chill into the marrow of her bones. Manning sat down in the chair with the lions' heads and watched her, tapping his foot. She caught his eye.

'Poor Gordon,' she said, and began to clear the room up,

folding the clothes away in drawers, hanging the dried shirts up in the wardrobe, and sliding the suitcases beneath the bed.

'Oh, dear,' said Proctor-Gould when he returned, looking round for the piles of clothing beneath which the Nescafé and the mugs lived. He dropped to his knees and pulled the suitcases out from under the bed.

'I keep telling them not to touch anything,' he said, 'but they keep tidying everything away.'

Manning laughed, looking at Raya.

'It's an obsession some people have,' went on Proctor-Gould, mistaking the reason for Manning's laughter. Manning laughed again.

They watched in silence while Proctor-Gould levered the lid off the tin, measured out the apostle spoons of brown powder, and added the cooling water from the camper's kettle. In silence they stirred their mugs and sipped at them, unable to think of anything to say to each other. Proctor-Gould took up his position with his back to the radiator, gazing sombrely down at the toe-caps of his shoes, moving his eyebrows thoughtfully up and down. Manning stared into space. Raya walked about the room, touching pieces of furniture, putting her head on one side and examining the stacks of English books on the table. Once she looked suddenly down into her mug after she had taken a mouthful and asked Manning curiously:

'What is it?'

'Coffee.'

Then they relapsed into silence again.

'Well,' said Manning at last, 'we must be going. I should think Raya's probably missed her last bus already.'

'That's all right. She can sleep here.'

'What?'

'Why not?'

In his astonishment Manning could think only of a practical reason.

'What about the floor-clerk?'

Proctor-Gould laughed, and pulled at his ear.

'I see,' he said. 'I thought for a moment that your indignation was based on moral grounds.'

'It is. So will the floor-clerk's be.'

'Will you translate, please?' said Raya. 'I know you're arguing about me again.'

'I don't think we need worry about the floor-clerk,' said Proctor-Gould. 'The authorities are much more sensible and understanding than you'd suppose.'

'What does that mean?'

'I mean they seem to realize that the sort of job I'm doing sometimes involves contacts with people in rather unusual circumstances.'

'In other words, you've done this before?'

'Done what before, Paul?'

'Had women up here.'

'Are you *asking* me?'

'Yes, I am.'

'That's not the sort of question you usually ask your friends, is it?'

'I'm just interested to know whether Raya's the thirtieth or only, say, the tenth.'

'Please,' cried Raya, 'what are you two jackasses saying?'

Neither of them replied. They were walking about the room not looking at each other.

'Look, Paul,' said Proctor-Gould in a concessive tone. 'You know as well as I do that when a foreigner stays at a hotel in Moscow he's rung up by prostitutes.'

'You've had prostitutes up here?'

'Purely for business reasons.' He realized what he had said and gave a little giggle. 'Perhaps that's a rather unfortunate way of putting it. I mean, purely to see if they would do as clients for me.'

'How did you make assignments with them? You can't speak Russian.'

'I know the Russian for "yes, please," Paul.'

'You've invited prostitutes up here late at night, sat them down in this arm-chair, given them cups of Nescafé, looked them over to see if they would do as personalities, then politely bowed them out again?'

'More or less. I paid them, of course.'

'But you couldn't even *talk* to them!'

'We just used to smile and make gestures.'

'You sat here smiling and making gestures?'

'Yes.'

'Drinking Nescafé?'

'Yes.'

'In silence?'

'I sometimes had the radio on.'

'Well, God help me!'

'Do you believe me?'

Manning stared at him.

'I suppose I do,' he said. 'I suppose I do.'

'I must admit, it wasn't very satisfactory. It was one of the jobs I wanted you for.'

'Will you please tell me what's going on?' cried Raya.

'You can't imagine how maddening it is to be left in the dark while this sort of argument flashes about one's head.'

They looked round. They had both forgotten about her.

'He's inviting you to sleep here,' said Manning briefly.

'That's very kind of him,' she replied. 'Yes, please.'

'I wish you'd stop trying to irritate me,' said Manning. 'Come on. I'll see you to a taxi.'

'She accepted my invitation, didn't she?' said Proctor-Gould.

'Look, don't be stupid,' said Manning. 'Anyway, what about your rule?'

'What rule?'

'I thought you had a rule about not getting emotionally involved while you were over here?'

'Who said anything about getting emotionally involved, Paul?'

'If spending the night with people isn't getting emotionally involved with them . . . '

'Don't leap to conclusions, Paul. I shall doss down in the arm-chair. There's no question of getting *involved* in any way at all.'

'What about the danger of blackmail?'

'Blackmail, Paul?'

'You were warning me about it, if you remember.'

'Good heavens Paul! You don't think *Raya*'s a police spy, do you?'

'Well, we don't know, do we?'

'I don't think that's a very chivalrous attitude, Paul.'

'Gordon, three days ago it was *your* attitude!'

'At that stage I hadn't met Raya. I was speaking generally. If there's one thing I've learnt in life, Paul, it's that success goes to the man who knows when to modify his general principles to meet the situation in hand.'

'You really have tumbled head over heels, haven't you, Gordon!'

'Paul, there's no question of tumbling head over heels, or any involvement of any sort whatsoever. I'm just offering Raya somewhere to sleep for the night because she's almost certainly missed her last bus.'

'Gordon, let's not delude ourselves. You're in love with Raya.'

'Certainly not.'

'Oh, Gordon! You're making a pass at her! I may say it's the most preposterous, clumsy, witless pass I've ever seen made.'

'Paul, let me assure you I have no designs upon Raya.'

'Let me tell you something, Gordon. You're the archetype of a certain sort of impotence. . . . '

'Now, Paul, let's not raise our voices. . . . '

'You flirt with other men's women. You get prostitutes in and pay them for drinking Nescafé. . . . '

'Now, come, come, Paul. . . . '

'You launch into little adventures where there's no possibility of failure because there's no possibility of success. . . .'

There was a sharp rap on the door. They swung round. The old woman from the floor-clerk's desk was standing on the threshold.

'Quieter! Quieter!' she whispered furiously. 'It's after midnight – you'll wake the whole hotel!'

After she had gone Manning and Proctor-Gould stood for a moment looking at each other in silence.

'Well,' said Manning, 'Raya and I are going.'

He looked round to tell her. But she had vanished. She had disappeared from the room without trace.

It was Proctor-Gould who saw her first. She was in bed, with the covers drawn up over her nose, apparently fast asleep. Propped up against the carafe of water on the bedside was one of her playing cards. On it was written in her childish ballpoint hand:

'A call at 8.0 a.m., please, with cheese, fruit, sour milk, and coffee.'

16

Manning spent a good deal of the night walking up and down his room in Sector B, his fists clenched, unable to believe that he had been treated so badly.

'I can't believe it!' he said to himself aloud over and over again, raising his eyebrows and running his hand through his hair, until the window was grey with dawn, and he was too exhausted to remember what it was that he couldn't believe. When he woke up two or three hours later he could believe it even less, and when, as he sat haggard and sleepy in the Faculty Library, he received the usual message that Proctor-Gould had phoned and asked him to go over to the hotel, it seemed to him that his impressions of what had taken place the previous evening had simply been mistaken, and that nothing had really changed at all.

But it had. Even as he opened the door of Proctor-Gould's room he noticed the smell was different. It no longer smelt of loneliness and soiled white shirts – a smell which Manning had always found bleak but curiously English. Instead there was a mixture of warm, cheerful smells – Russian cigarettes, scent, hot cloth. And the appearance of the room had changed. There was a vase of tulips on the chest of drawers, a bowl of birch twigs on the escritoire. The stacks of books had been arranged neatly on shelves, and several large pictures had been pinned to the wall. They were of doll-like figures with red cheeks holding single flowers in their hands, childishly painted in bright poster colours on sheets of dark art paper. The piles of dirty linen and the open suitcases had gone. So had the washing with which the room had on previous occasions been festooned. Instead, Manning noticed, a blanket from the bed had been spread over one of the Imperial occasional tables, leaving the clawed golden feet of the table sticking out ridiculously from underneath, like the boots of a lover hiding behind a curtain in a French farce. On the blanket stood a neat stack of folded pyjamas and shirts, and an up-ended electric iron which clicked as it cooled and contracted.

By comparison with the changed décor, Proctor-Gould and Raya themselves seemed surprisingly familiar. To Manning their ordinariness was depressing; the new *status quo* was not a matter of impression or interpretation at all, but common, objective fact. Proctor-Gould stood with his back to the radiator, pulling at his ear. Raya lay on top of the bed, propped up on her elbow. It was as if they had always been so, as if a world which contained them in any other way was inconceivable.

'Welcome to our little nest,' said Raya, shaking the hair out of her eyes. 'It's not much, but it's home.'

Manning was embarrassed. So evidently was Proctor-Gould, though he seemed highly pleased with himself as well. He kept frowning importantly to hide his pleasure, and pulling harder and harder at his ear.

'You'll have it right off if you're not careful,' said Manning irritably. Proctor-Gould began to giggle at once, and went on for a long time. Manning noticed that his blazer had been brushed and his trousers were pressed. The pens and pencils had been removed from his breast pocket. He looked almost sleek.

'Do you like the pictures?' Proctor-Gould asked at last.

'Very nice.'

'Raya painted them herself.'

'Really?'

'At least, I think she did. I think that's what she was saying.'

There was an awkward silence.

'The point is, Paul,' said Proctor-Gould, 'we need to get a few things settled as between Raya and myself.'

'I suppose you do.'

'I wondered whether you would be kind enough to interpret for us?'

'What?'

'I hope you don't mind?'

'Oh, for God's sake . . .!'

'What do you mean, Paul?'

'I mean – well, for God's sake . . .!'

Proctor-Gould pulled at his ear again.

'I see your point, Paul,' he said. 'But I can scarcely get one of the Intourist interpreters up, can I? Look, I shan't ask you to translate anything that might embarrass you. There are just one or two little logistical points we ought to get straight. I've been trying to get through to her all day in sign language, but we haven't made much headway.'

'She's been here all day?'

'She disappeared after breakfast – I thought for good.

But when I came up to have a nap and a cup of Nescafé after lunch she was back, and she'd brought all this stuff with her.'

He gazed round the room at her handiwork. He seemed pleased and proud, but a little out of his depth.

'Very nice,' said Manning. 'But when's she going? You're not thinking of letting her stay tonight, are you?'

'That's rather what I want to establish. I think she's fetched her pyjamas.'

'Look, don't be stupid. You can't just set up with a mistress in the best hotel in Moscow.'

'I know, I know,' said Proctor-Gould. He began to walk up and down the room, his hands behind his back, frowning anxiously. Raya watched him from the bed, and lit a cigarette.

'Let me know what conclusions you arrive at, gentlemen,' she said.

'What did she say?' asked Proctor-Gould at once.

'Asked to be told our conclusions.'

'Ah. She said quite a lot this afternoon. I couldn't get a word of it.'

'I expect somebody got it.'

'How do you mean?'

Manning pointed at the wall and mimed speaking into a microphone. 'You've thought of that aspect?' he asked.

'Microphones? Oh, yes.'

'You don't mind the prospect of being blackmailed?'

'Paul, we went into all this last night.'

'We never arrived at any sense.'

'Look, Paul, I'm entirely in the hands of the Soviet authorities anyway. If they want to find a lever against me, or an excuse for expelling me, they don't have to mess about with footling misdemeanours like having a guest in my room after hours. All they've got to do is to get one of my clients to say I'd tried to persuade him to work for British Intelligence.'

'All the same, if you insist on forcing your moral ideas on their attention they may feel compelled to do something about it.'

'Exactly, Paul, exactly. The problem, as in all things in life, is to find the acceptable mean. That's why I want you to help me in clarifying the situation.'

'You want me to tell Raya to remove herself?'

'No, no, no. I want us all to sit down to a round-table conference and discuss the situation like sensible people.'

Manning looked at Raya. She looked gravely back at him. He supposed that he should want to turn his back on her and never see her again. But he felt a great desire to remain in the same room as her, on any terms whatever. Besides, her decision to move in on Proctor-Gould was no doubt a pure caprice. It would pass, and she would return to him as suddenly and strangely as she had abandoned him, provided he was still at hand.

'All right,' said Manning. 'Just this once. Don't think I shall come running every time you crook your finger.'

'Of course not,' said Proctor-Gould. 'Once we've got these few basic points straightened out we shan't need you, anyway.'

Manning pointed at the table in the centre of the room. 'Round-table conference,' he said to Raya. At once she sprang off the bed and set a chair for herself.

Now that the moment for communication had come, Proctor-Gould seemed suddenly abstracted. He sat down at the table, but almost immediately stood up again, and cleared his throat.

'Firstly . . .' he began.

'For God's sake,' said Manning. 'Sit down.'

'Ah,' said Proctor-Gould, sitting down, but not abandoning the sleepwalker's air that men have when they are about to tell a joke or make a speech.

'Firstly, Paul,' he began again, and the slightly hesitant way in which he said 'Paul' made it sound like a special concession to informality, 'will you tell Raya what very great pleasure it gives me to have her here in this room?'

Manning winced, and Proctor-Gould at once began to giggle and pull at his ear

'I hope I can rely on you, Paul,' he said humorously, 'to remove any unfortunate double meanings as you translate.'

'He's glad you're here,' said Manning to Raya.

'I'm glad I'm here, too,' said Raya. She got up and kissed Proctor-Gould on the ear. He put his arm round her and giggled again.

'What did she say?' he asked.

'Glad to be here.'

'Tell her I think she's an absolute sweetie,' demanded Proctor-Gould, giving her hips a squeeze, and rubbing his hand briskly up and down her further thigh, as if to restore circulation.

'Oh, shut up.'

'Go on, tell her.'

'It's not a logistical point.'

Proctor-Gould thought about this for some time in silence. Then he gave Raya's thigh a couple of final rubs.

'I suppose not,' he said. 'Let's get back to business, then.'

He gave Raya a dismissive pat on the bottom, rested his elbows on the table, clasped his hands together, and leaned forward with a serious air.

'Now, the first point is this,' he said, hammering it into the air with his clasped hands. 'Can we establish what Raya's plans are? Does she intend to remain here tonight?'

Manning translated.

'Yes,' said Raya.

'Well, of course,' said Proctor-Gould, 'I'm very pleased. Delightful. Now could you, Paul, with the utmost tact, find out approximately – or even exactly – how long she intends to remain after tonight? Is she anxious to get home tomorrow? Or would she want to stay, say, another night? But put it with the utmost delicacy.'

'How long are you staying altogether?' translated Manning.

'Until we are tired of each other.'

'I see,' said Proctor-Gould when Manning had translated it to him. 'Yes. I see that. But do you think she realizes the position she may be putting herself in *vis-à-vis* the authorities?'

'Of course she does. If she didn't have some understanding with the authorities she wouldn't be here in the first place.'

'Ask her anyway.'

Raya shrugged.

'Why ask, Paul? I know you've always thought I was a police spy.'

'Look, Raya, you must have some understanding with someone or you wouldn't be here, would you?'

'Why not?'

'Because you'd get into trouble.'

'I might. I might not.'

'You'd be mad to risk it.'

'That depends how one wants to live. In this country one has only two alternatives. Either one must behave with an absolutely scrupulous regard for one's personal safety; or else one must totally ignore it and do exactly as one pleases, in the hope that one will be thought to be a member of some different species, not subject to the rules at all.'

Manning stared at her, absolutely undecided what to think about her. She looked pleased by his uncertainty, as uncompromising as any god in her refusal to dispel his doubt by supernatural demonstration.

'Give poor Gordon some sort of report on the conversation,' she ordered. 'He's looking terribly worried.'

Manning reported, and Proctor-Gould leaned forward

across the table to listen, his brown eyes very wide open, his thumb and index finger fondling the lobe of his ear incessantly.

'Ah,' he said when Manning had finished. 'I go part of the way with Raya. But I think that if one is flouting the generally accepted rules of behaviour one must exercise discretion. Undoubtedly the authorities know that Raya is here. If last night's anything to go by, they seem to be prepared to overlook it. But we must make it easy for them to overlook it. We must make sure that we don't create a public scandal which could be ignored only by deliberate choice. We must limit ourselves to an inconspicuous irregularity which people could argue afterwards, if they were challenged, was merely overlooked in error.

'Now, here is my schedule of regulations, if Raya is to stay. One: she must leave the room in the morning, separately from me. Two: she must not normally come up to the room during the day while I am out of it. Three: she must not leave her personal possessions lying about. Four: she must not be seen taking meals with me in the hotel restaurant. Five: if anyone knocks on the door while she is in the room she must withdraw to the bathroom.'

Manning translated these conditions to Raya in his most neutral voice, waiting to be interrupted at each moment by the laughter with which she would greet them. But she did not laugh. She sat doodling abstractedly on a piece of paper she had found on the table, saying nothing, with no expression on her face. It irritated Manning to watch her. He realized gloomily that he had never at any time even begun to understand her, and he suddenly doubted that he ever would.

'Well?' said Proctor-Gould to Manning.
'He says "Well?"' translated Manning to Raya.
She sighed.
'Would it really make Gordon happy if I agreed to all these conditions?' she asked.

Manning inquired.

'If Raya would agree to stay on the terms I have mentioned,' said Proctor-Gould, his great brown eyes very wide, 'it would be both a matter of personal satisfaction to me and, I think, a very valuable and interesting experiment in co-existence at the personal level.'

When Manning had translated this to Raya she held up her drawing for them to see. It was a girl doll, like the ones around the walls. Her peg limbs were bent in a ridiculous curtsy, and in a balloon from her mouth were the two letters EC, followed by an exclamation mark.

'What does EC mean?' asked Proctor-Gould.

'I don't know. It's not Russian.'

He frowned, trying over the two Cyrillic letters on his tongue.

'"Ye-S",' he repeated stupidly. '"Yes." "Yes." "Yes." I don't know.'

Proctor-Gould watched him patiently, waiting for him to decipher it. But the paper was shaking about in front of Manning's eyes. Raya was laughing at them.

17

Manning and Katerina stopped on one of the bridges over the Moskva, and leaned on the parapet, looking absently down into the water. Behind them two-car trams ground slowly across from the city side to the eastern suburbs, still packed with people bound for the noisy dark courtyards and the shabby tenement stairs.

'I can see why Raya pleased you,' said Katerina. 'If I'd met her I might have been attracted to her, too.'

'Spiritually?'

'Perhaps physically as well. There's no real difference. All relationships are fundamentally political. One dominates;

one is dominated; one rules by consent. There's nothing mysterious about physical attraction. It's just an expression of one's desire for a particular form of political relationship.'

'I'm not sure that men always want to dominate, or women to be dominated.'

'I agree. Or perhaps one might say that some men are women, and some women are men. You and I are two of the world's natural women. We love people because of what makes them people – their will and their freedom – and we expect to be used ourselves as objects – as the raw material on which the volition of others is exercised. Raya must be a natural man. She uses you. She uses Proctor-Gould. She does it not by strength or command, but by caprice, by taunting you and teasing you. It amounts to the same thing. You both delight in being used. So should I if the situation had arisen.'

'The strong and the weak again.'

'Yes. Kanysh is a natural man. He had a tiny room in a block off Baumann Street. I used to visit him when he wanted me to; stay away when he wanted me to. If he chose, we would sit in silence for a whole afternoon, he sitting on the end of the bed, I in the only chair. He would sit with his head in his hands, thinking his own thoughts. I would sit watching him, labouring to think not my thoughts but his. Or he would tell me about his life. Not for me to break in and say: "Yes, yes, I know exactly how you must have felt. When I was a child . . ." and so on, as people do. But for me just to listen, scarcely daring to breathe, while he talked on and on about the wrongs and sufferings which obsessed him, hardly noticing I was there. Or else he would make me tell him about my life, so that he could wrap it about his own wounds – the way country people do with cobwebs. That's how I felt my life was on those days – cobweb, a nothing, thin shreds of nothing. But enough to give him some consolation. We never had a conversation, in the way that you and I have conversations, each giving and each taking, treating each other as free and equal beings. I should have hated that with him. Perhaps he depended on me – but only like one depends upon potatoes and bread. He was subject and I was object. It was absolute and complete. You and I – we're hopeless. Just two runaway slaves – two women away from their men, chattering on companionably and vacuously, getting nothing done. But it's cosy. I like it, Paul. . . .'

She was crying. Manning put his hand on her arm.

'Oh, Katya,' he said. 'Don't cry, Katya.'

She wiped her eyes on a large crumpled handkerchief, and blew her nose clumsily.

'Kanysh hasn't written to me for three weeks now,' she said. 'I think he's in trouble. I don't know. I just have a feeling that something's happened.'

She took a deep breath, stopped crying, and put the handkerchief away. They began to walk again.

Just in front of them was a man with a shaven head, carrying a small, broken attaché-case. He walked more and more slowly, as if he was coming to the end of a journey. At the great bend in the street beyond the bridge, where the trams came grinding round on the curve, he stopped, set his bag down on the pavement beside him, and gazed at the district ahead. Manning looked at his face in the light from the street lamps as they passed him. There was no expression on it, but his head slowly turned, his eyes taking in everything before him. Inch by inch he examined it all – the bend in the street, a blank wooden fence with missing boards, a shuttered kiosk, two concrete telegraph standards at slightly different angles to the vertical – as if he was recognizing a place seen in a dream. A man returning. From where? After how long? With nothing but what would go into that small attaché-case? The prodigies and portents of Manning's walks with Katya. Manning turned round and looked again just before they lost him to sight round the bend. He was still standing there, still gazing.

18

Raya remained in Proctor-Gould's room, her presence unchallenged by the hotel, the police, or anyone else. The floor clerk nodded at her when she came in and went out, the chambermaid folded her pyjamas and put them beneath the pillow. Otherwise no one remarked on her existence at all. To Proctor-Gould's code of rules she paid not the slightest attention, coming and going from the room when she chose, arranging her belongings neatly on top of the chest of drawers and in the bathroom, and if she felt like it silently accompanying Proctor-Gould to the restaurant for dinner.

Proctor-Gould became increasingly preoccupied. In the middle of a rather difficult lunch with some officials of the Moscow public health department he leaned over to Manning and said in a low voice:

'*Bolvan.*'

'What?'

'What does it mean? "Darling"? "Sweetheart"?'

'It means "numbskull".'

'Ah.'

There was less and less for Manning to interpret between Proctor-Gould and his official contacts, more and more between him and Raya. Manning's earnings declined; it was somehow tacitly agreed between them that it would be improper for Manning to be paid for interpreting Proctor-Gould's dealings with his mistress. Each day Manning swore that he would have nothing more to do with them; but each time the message came he hurried round, certain that this time she was going to leave him.

They were an odd couple, and became no less odd as time went on. They quarrelled endlessly, with Manning's assistance, chiefly about Raya's failure to observe the regulations Proctor-Gould had laid down. Or rather, Proctor-

Gould quarrelled, and she did not, like one hand clapping.

'Will you tell her,' Proctor-Gould would say with a curious mixture of indulgence and exasperation, 'that when I came up after lunch today I found the bath full of underwear and stockings to soak?'

'Tell him I'm sorry,' Raya would reply.

'She's *always* sorry. Now, point one, she must have come back to the room in her free period, between eleven and twelve. Point two, the chambermaid must have seen those things in the bath. Now I know Raya often comes back to the room while I'm out, though she won't admit it, and I know the chambermaid can see two pairs of high-heeled shoes in the wardrobe anyway. But it's the *principle* of the thing. Can you try and make that clear to her?'

Raya would solemnly promise not to do it again.

'She promises?' Proctor-Gould would cry despairingly when this had been translated. 'But she *always* promises. Every day she lies there on the bed and solemnly promises not to do whatever she has been doing. And every day she continues to do it just the same.'

'I don't see what more I can do,' Raya would tell Manning regretfully. 'I've given my solemn word of honour.'

'I think this time he wants you to keep it.'

'All right. I give my solemn word of honour that this time I will keep my solemn word of honour.'

It was, thought Manning, the consistent failure of his attempts to deal with her by means of reason which were visibly debilitating Proctor-Gould. He was a man who believed deeply in the reasonableness of reason.

Manning wondered whether they made love at night. They certainly shared the bed. He found it difficult to imagine them so helpless and exposed before each other. But then, thought Manning, it was difficult to imagine anybody one knew socially engaged in the sincere and serious labour of intercourse. There were less likely couples than Proctor-Gould and Raya. Not many. But some.

In spite of everything, Proctor-Gould still refused all Manning's suggestions that Raya should move out. 'I'm not sure that she'd go even if I told her to,' he said – and the thought made him giggle. Manning suspected that he took a certain pleasure in being so helpless in her hands. He was proud to possess her, and proud that she was so untamed by possession, like a man who is pleased with his new car because it goes fast enough to frighten him.

Soon she went even faster. She began to steal his belongings.

At first Proctor-Gould didn't guess it was her.

'Paul,' he said one afternoon, in a puzzled voice. 'You remember that silver skyscraper Professor Kornyukov gave me at the History Faculty reception? Well, it's gone.'

'Gone?'

'It was with some other presents in the bottom of the chest of drawers. Now it's vanished. I've searched the whole room. Not a sign of it.'

'Have you reported it to the management?'

'Not yet. Do you think I should, Paul? I mean, the situation in this room being what it is?'

'I don't know.'

'Ask Raya what she thinks.'

Manning asked her.

'She doesn't think it's really necessary to report it,' he told Proctor-Gould.

'Doesn't she?'

'No. She took it herself.'

Proctor-Gould stared at her, or at any rate at the top of her head, since she was bending over one of his shirts, sewing a button on.

'What's she done with it, then, Paul?'

'She says she's sold it.'

Raya looked up and saw Proctor-Gould frowning at her and pulling at his ear.

'Tell him I bought the dress I've got on at the moment

with the proceeds,' she said to Manning. 'The trouble with your friend Gordon is that he doesn't notice what I'm wearing.'

'Tell her,' said Proctor-Gould, 'tell her ... Well, I don't know. I'm not sure what you'd better tell her.'

Next day she stole all the other presents in the drawer.

'Gordon couldn't possibly have *wanted* all that junk, could he?' she asked Manning, when he arrived to translate at the subsequent inquiry.

'The people in England I was supposed to be taking it back to might have liked it,' said Proctor-Gould heavily. 'But seriously, Paul, what on earth is she up to? The silver skyscraper might have been worth something. But the rest of the stuff can't have fetched more than five or six roubles together.'

The following day it became rather more serious.

'Will you ask her if she knows anything about the whereabouts of my Nescafé?' Proctor-Gould asked Manning, putting on his most humorously patient expression.

'Does it really matter?' said Manning. 'The tin was almost empty.'

'*That* tin was,' conceded Proctor-Gould with a little ironic bow. 'But there were five more tins in the wardrobe – enough to see me through the whole trip.'

'They've gone, too?'

'Every one. I've been miming sipping, then opening the wardrobe and raising my eyebrows, but all she does it fetch glasses of tea from the old woman down the corridor. Then she locks them in the wardrobe and raises *her* eyebrows.'

Manning put the matter to Raya.

'Oh, the coffee powder,' she said. 'Yes, I found all those unwanted tins of coffee powder in the wardrobe this morning, so I took them out and sold them to a friend of mine. Coffee powder fetches a lot of money in Moscow.'

Proctor-Gould stared gloomily at the floor for a long time when Manning translated this to him, no doubt wondering how he was going to put up with Raya for the rest of his stay without Nescafé to console him. With the money from the Nescafé Raya bought a black-market copy of *Dr Zhivago*. Proctor-Gould's distress must have touched her, though, for she stole a volume of Nekrasov he had been given by the Art Literature Publishing House and bought back one of the tins of Nescafé, which she gave to him and made up whenever he wanted.

'It's got to stop,' he told Manning, sipping at a cup which Raya had brought him unbidden. 'I'm not joking, Paul. It can't go on.'

He looked nervous. How Raya looked Manning could not tell. She was lying on her stomach on the bed, reading *Dr Zhivago*, her hair hanging down around the book like a curtain.

'I suppose it's intended as a practical joke, is it?' demanded Proctor-Gould. 'The Slavonic sense of humour?'

'I don't know, I'm afraid,' said Manning.

'I thought you were the great expert on the Slavonic temperament?'

'I thought you were?'

'I don't understand the first thing about these people,' said Proctor-Gould morosely.

It was the first time that Manning had seen him really depressed.

19

The next time Proctor-Gould sought Manning's help with Raya it was nothing to do with either an infraction of the rules or theft. They were in the Chaika, being driven back from a meeting.

'Paul,' said Proctor-Gould suddenly, after a long silence, 'May I ask your advice on a rather ticklish point?'

'Ask away.'

'It's about Raya.'

For some time Proctor-Gould did not take the matter any further. He sat pulling at his ear, and looking out of the window.

'What is it, then?' asked Manning.

'It's rather awkward. I don't know quite how to put it.'

He sighed. Manning suddenly had the idea that he was going to ask him to take Raya off his hands.

'You were quite a chum of hers at one time, weren't you?' said Proctor-Gould.

Manning looked out of the window as well.

'I suppose you might put it like that,' he said.

'I mean, I realize you think I'm rather a bastard, having to some extent horned in on you.'

'No, no. . . .'

'Of course you do. It's only natural. I should feel exactly the same in your place.'

'Honestly, Gordon, there's no need to feel . . .'

'I mean, I know all's fair in love and war . . .'

'Gordon, there's really no need to feel, you know . . .'

'You mean, you don't feel, well . . .?'

'Of course not, Gordon. I mean, there's no need to feel you know. . .'

'Really? Well, I appreciate that, Paul. It shows a generous spirit, and I appreciate it.'

'I mean . . .'

'No, no. I appreciate it.'

They became silent again. They had both been looking at the back of the chauffeur's head as they spoke, and they both now looked out of the windows again.

'What I was going to say, as a matter of fact, Paul,' resumed Proctor-Gould finally, 'was – well – you were rather a pal of Raya's, weren't you?'

'A great pal.'

'Yes. Well. The point is, can you remember if she is – what shall I say? – suitably equipped?'

'How do you mean, suitably equipped?'

Proctor-Gould essayed a man-to-man laugh.

'You know,' he said.

'No?'

Proctor-Gould stopped laughing.

'I mean,' he said heavily, 'does she take proper precautions in these cases against the possible consequences?'

At last Manning saw. He was so surprised that he uttered a little squeaking gasp of laughter.

'God knows,' said Proctor-Gould. 'It's an awkward thing to have to ask you. I appreciate that. But I'm in a rather tricky position. I didn't bring any with me. Stupid of me, I see now, but it simply didn't occur to me. And not speaking the language, I don't quite see how to go about getting any.'

'I suppose not.'

'And of course I can't ask her, either.'

'No.'

'It's not the sort of thing you can really manage in sign-language.'

'I see your point.'

'And it has always been an inflexible rule of mine not to try any monkey business without some reliable form of contraceptive.'

'Very sensible.'

'I mean, when the occasion has arisen. I wouldn't put myself down as a great Don Juan. But when the occasion has arisen ...'

'Quite.'

There was a silence. Proctor-Gould worked on his ear again, looking out of the window.

'So,' he said finally, 'did she?'

'What?'

'Raya. Did she ...?'

'Oh. I don't know.'

'You didn't . . .?'

'I'm afraid not.'

'I'm sorry. I thought you were great pals.'

'Not as great as all that.'

'No. I see. I'm sorry.'

They were silent again until the car was quite near the hotel.

'Well, then,' said Proctor-Gould, 'I'll ask the driver to stop at the next chemist's we pass. Perhaps you'd pop in and get me a packet.'

'No.'

'No?'

'I don't even know the Russian.'

Proctor-Gould sighed, and fell silent again. As the car pulled up in front of the hotel he made one last attempt.

'Well,' he said, 'perhaps you'll just slip upstairs and ask her.'

'Now, Gordon. . . .'

'Even if you don't know the exact word you could paraphrase it.'

'Don't be ridiculous, Gordon.'

'If you think my presence might embarrass you I'll wait downstairs.'

'No.'

The commissionaire was holding the door open.

'This makes things most awkward for me,' said Proctor-Gould.

'You'll just have to restrain yourself.'

'It's not really a question of me restraining myself,' said Proctor-Gould, looking gloomier than ever. 'It's what she's going to do.'

He left Manning on the pavement, and disappeared into the hotel. It seemed to Manning, as he watched him go, that his shoulders were visibly bowed.

20

Pulled by the strange centripetal force that cities have, Manning and Katerina ended up, as they usually did, on Mokhovaya Street in front of the old university. For some time they had said nothing. Katerina looked ill. She sat down on the low wall which the drunken man had fallen over, and admitted that she felt sick and dizzy with hunger.

'Did you have any lunch today?' asked Manning.

She shook her head.

'Now that's *stupid*, isn't it, Katya?'

'I didn't feel like it at the time.'

'We've been through all this before.'

'I've told you – I've never eaten much. When Kanysh was here I couldn't eat knowing he was hungry.'

'Anyway, let's go and have a proper meal somewhere now.'

She shook her head again.

'Come on.'

'I honestly don't want to, Paul.'

'Now be sensible.'

'Don't try to bully me, Paul. You know you can't.'

Manning looked at her helplessly.

'You must have something,' he said, irresolute.

For a long time she didn't reply, but sat with her head in her hands, looking at the pavement. Then she gave a long sigh, and stood up.

'If we can go somewhere quiet I'll come and watch you eat. I might have some soup.'

'How about the Faculty canteen? It'll be empty at this time of night.'

Katerina thought, turning her lower lip over doubtfully with her index finger.

'I haven't got my pass with me,' she said at last.

'I've got mine. They'll let you in with me. I don't suppose there'll be anyone on the door now.'

But, as they shortly discovered, there was. The same old woman with the crooked glasses, sitting on the same broken chair.

'No one can come in here without a pass,' she said.

'She's forgotten it,' said Manning. 'What does it matter?'

'No one can come in here without a pass.'

'Oh, never mind,' said Katerina, flushing. 'Let's go to an Automat instead.'

'No,' said Manning, beginning to lose his temper. 'Now we're here we're going in.'

He turned back to the old woman.

'Look, she's a member of the Philological Faculty. She's got a pass, but she's forgotten it. I'll vouch for her.'

'She can't come in without a pass.'

'Well, I'm afraid she's going to.'

'Paul, *please* don't make a scene!' begged Katerina. She was wringing her hands in misery.

'Come on, Katya. We're going in.'

'*Please*, Paul!'

'I'll call the Dean!' cried the old woman.

'Call him, then! We'll be in the canteen.'

But at that moment the dispute abruptly ceased. All three of them had become simultaneously aware that the Dean was already present. It was a creak on the stairs that they had heard. They turned, and there stood Korolenko, on the creaky eleventh stair, silently watching them. They gazed back, their mouths open as if to speak, the speech evaporated.

Every one was afraid of Korolenko. He was a neatly-built, shortish man, and he carried himself with the un-exaggerated correctness of a born professional soldier. His head was bald, and gleamed like a polished helmet in the light over the stairs. His cheeks were sunken, his mouth set in a precise line. His features were completely immobile, apart from a tic which drew the right-hand corner of his mouth up from time to time, as if in a brief ironic smile. Perhaps it *was* an ironic smile. The complete stillness, the soldier's willed passivity, from which the spasm surfaced, concealed his nature like a suit of armour. It was surprising he had moved enough to make the stair creak.

They stared at him, hypnotized, waiting for him to speak first. When he did, it was to say something that Manning found very surprising.

'Katerina Fyodorovna Lippe,' he said, without expression of any sort.

He knew her.

Manning glanced at her. She was looking down, as if bowed before him.

'Did I hear this young man say that you had forgotten your pass?' asked Korolenko in the same voice.

Katerina said nothing.

'You have no pass, Lippe. You have no right to enter any part of the university.'

Katerina looked up.

'Now, that's not correct, Igor Viktorovich,' she said pleadingly.

'You were expelled from the post-graduate school of the Philological Faculty three years ago. Since then you've had no connexion with the university.'

'Igor Viktorovich, you know that's not true!'

Katerina's voice had risen imploringly, and her eyes were filled with tears.

'You come back to haunt us.'

'Igor Viktorovich!'

'You hang around the university like a lost dog. Have you no work to do? No home to go back to?'

'*Please*, Igor Viktorovich!'

'You fasten yourself upon people like our English comrade here and fill them up with slanders about our university, about our country.'

'No! That's not true! Don't say things like that! Please don't say things like that!'

Katerina had gone very red in the face, and her voice broke. She sounded as if she was unable to catch her breath. Korolenko, on the other hand, had remained completely impassive. Now he turned to Manning, and the corner of his mouth twitched up, as if ironically deprecating an unpleasant necessity.

'You must excuse us,' he said. 'A small domestic matter. No doubt you have similar problems at English universities.'

'Look,' said Manning, 'I must make it clear at once that never on any occasion have I heard Katerina say anything critical or disloyal.'

'I'm glad to hear it,' replied Korolenko. 'She has a record of negative contribution.'

The mouth twitched sardonically up again, and he turned to the doorkeeper.

'She was creating a disturbance here tonight?'

'She was trying to get in without a pass.'

'Quite.'

'It's my responsibility entirely,' said Manning. 'I invited her to eat in the canteen.'

'I see,' said Korolenko. 'As you will no doubt recall, the canteen is not open to members of the general public.'

'I'm sorry. We'll go somewhere else.'

'However, we shouldn't like you to take away an impression of inflexibility or over-zealous adherence to the rules. So on this occasion I will waive them.'

Manning looked at Katerina. She was screwing her handkerchief around in her hands in anguish, and two tears were running down her cheeks.

'I think we'd prefer to go away and eat somewhere else now,' said Manning.

'No, no, no,' said Korolenko. 'I insist.'

'I think . . .'

'As my guests. I will give instructions for the bill to be sent up to me.'

Manning looked at Katerina uncertainly. She would not catch his eye.

'Please don't mention it,' said Korolenko, as they hesitated in silence. '*Bon appetit.*'

He remained on the eleventh stair, watching them. Propelled by his unblinking gaze, they walked slowly across the lobby to the head of the basement stairs, and went down to the canteen. The smell of grease and cabbage rose around them. Inside, the bare bulbs shone on a glass case with three round yellow cakes in it, and on one solitary student at a table, sitting with his elbows on the dirty oilcloth, gulping down soup.

Manning fetched bowls of soup and glasses of tea from the counter. But Katerina would not touch hers. Several times it was on the tip of his tongue to ask her how she knew Korolenko, and whether she had really been expelled. But he did not, and Katerina volunteered nothing. She sat pale and strained, her eyes cast down, saying nothing, nothing at all, waiting only for Manning to finish and escort her past the doorkeeper again.

21

What action Raya took upon Proctor-Gould's person Manning never discovered. But a day or two later she began to steal his books.

It seemed to affect Proctor-Gould worse than anything that had happened so far. When Manning arrived, summoned by an incoherent telephone message, he found him pacing slowly up and down the room with his hands behind his back, his face haggard with anxiety.

'Where is she?' asked Manning.

'In the bath,' said Proctor-Gould, nodding at the bathroom door.

'She's pinched some books now?'

'Yes. About ten, I think – all Russian ones. She just picked out all the books I've been given by people here to take back.'

'You're sure it's Raya who took them?'

'Pretty sure. When I came in this afternoon the books were all over the place. I noticed it at once, of course, and started to count them. Raya was lying on the bed here. She looked up straight away and watched me.'

'Doesn't she always look up when you come in?'

'Not necessarily. But this time she watched me very closely, as if she wanted to see exactly what my reaction was.'

'You think she stole them just to irritate you?'

'I suppose so,' said Proctor-Gould, pulling at his ear, his eyes absent. 'I suppose so.'

'And were you irritated?'

'Yes, I was. I shouted at her. Of course, she couldn't understand any of it.'

'So you want me to translate the gist of it to her now?'

'No, no. I don't want you to translate anything. The time for rational argument seems to have passed. I really just wanted you to advise me. What am I going to do?'

He flopped down into the arm-chair, and gazed mournfully into the unoccupied middle air. Manning felt sorry for him.

'Look, Gordon,' he said. 'Do you still feel any attraction to Raya?'

Proctor-Gould looked at Manning solemnly.

'I think she's the most wonderful girl I've ever met,' he said.

'Nothing that's happened in the past week or two changes your view?'

'Nothing at all. No one could be in my line of business

without realizing that human relationships are often exceedingly complex. Raya and I have a complex relationship. But then we're both complicated, difficult people. Could we really expect a simpler one?'

'But do you think Raya still feels whatever she used to feel for you?'

'I think so, Paul, I think so. You may not realize, just seeing us for odd moments, but we're as thick as thieves.'

'Really?'

'Oh, like two bugs in a rug.'

'Even though you can't say anything to each other except "Yes, please"?'

'We don't need to say anything to each other, Paul. We have that sort of relationship.'

Manning went over and knocked on the bathroom door.

'Are you thinking of coming out?' he asked.

'No,' said Raya.

'We're talking about you.'

'Good. My best wishes for the enterprise.'

Manning sat down opposite Proctor-Gould again.

'She says she's not thinking of coming out,' he reported.

'No, I don't suppose she'll be out for another hour yet. She's taken to retiring to the bath with a book from six to eight every evening.'

'Another little complexity.'

'A perfectly harmless one, Paul.'

'Oh, sure. I think you'll just have to get used to the idea that Raya pinches things, too.'

'Did she ever take anything of yours, Paul?'

'No.'

Proctor-Gould sighed.

'As a matter of fact,' he said, 'I did get reasonably acclimatized to the idea of her taking things like my souvenirs, or the Nescafé. I can see that different people express their relationships in different ways. But the books are quite another matter. The books are part of my work. A lot of them

aren't even mine – I was entrusted with them by my clients,
to deliver. I just *cannot* allow Raya to take them.'

'Do you want me to ask her what she did with the ones
she took, so that we can try and get them back?'

Proctor-Gould sighed again.

'I think we'd better let those go. What I really want to
do is to make absolutely certain that she doesn't take any
more.'

Eventually they got two of Proctor-Gould's suitcases out
of the wardrobe, packed all the books away into them, and
locked them.

'Supposing she finds the key?' asked Manning.

'She won't. I'll keep the key-ring chained to me twenty-
four hours a day.'

'She could force the locks fairly easily.'

'I don't think she'd do that, Paul. I don't think she'd be
prepared to go to any trouble. Do you?'

'I don't know. I thought you were the one who understood her?'

'Yes. Well, I don't think she'd go to the trouble of forcing
the locks.'

22

Proctor-Gould was right; Raya didn't go to the trouble of
forcing the locks. She took one of the suitcases and sold it as
it stood, locked.

Then she came back to the hotel for the other one.
Proctor-Gould met her, and the porter carrying the second
suitcase, as they stepped out of the lift in the lobby.

'I didn't think I could manage them both at once,' she
explained to Manning when he arrived. 'It didn't occur to
me to get the porter the first time. Stupid of me – we might
have avoided all this mess.'

She indicated the heap of books which Proctor-Gould had taken out of the case and spread over the floor, and which he was now desperately sorting through. He was in a terrible state. He had only just discovered that the suitcase he had saved was the second one, and that the other had gone already. He kept picking books up and dropping them, trying to work out which ones he had lost, biting his lower lip so that it bulged out first to the left and then to the right. He looked as if he was going to be sick.

'Has she *really* sold the case?' he asked Manning.

'So she says.'

'Who to?'

'She says a friend.'

'Tell her I'm going to the police this time.'

Manning told her.

'She says shall she phone room service for a policeman?' he reported.

At these words Proctor-Gould jumped to his feet and stared at Raya, his eyes very wide, leaning forward ridiculously as if to inspect her more closely. His face was unnaturally white. The joke had turned all his anxiety to rage.

'I'll shake you!' he said in a level, frightening voice. 'I'm going to have those books back. You treat me like ... as if I didn't exist. ... You think ... Well! I'll shake you!'

His voice trembled, and went very high. Manning was too taken aback to translate. But Proctor-Gould's tone and appearance had a remarkable enough effect on Raya by themselves. For a moment a slight smile appeared on her face – a silly smile of astonishment and fear. It was the first sign Manning had seen that she was not impregnable. Then she put her hand on Proctor-Gould's arm very softly.

'Gordon, Gordon,' she said quietly. 'Something can be arranged. Hush, Gordon, we'll arrange something. Nothing's so positive, nothing's so final.'

'I'm going to have those books back,' repeated Proctor-Gould shakily.

Raya took his hand and patted it, then put it to her lips and kissed the back of his fingers. She was like a mother soothing her child.

'Let's put all these books away in the case again,' she said coaxingly, as if Proctor-Gould had thrown his toys about in a tantrum.

'Don't touch those books!' shouted Proctor-Gould, unable to understand what she had said, and even at this moment of revelation misunderstanding her intentions. For an instant they became locked in a clumsy scuffling. Then Raya had given up, and sat down with her hands folded in her lap, while Proctor-Gould scrabbled the books up from the floor and dumped them in the case all anyhow, with jackets coming off and pages doubling up. He crammed down the lid, relocked it, and put the case back in the wardrobe.

'Now, the other suitcase,' he said. The hot flush of adrenalin through his arteries had evidently passed. He sounded merely surly, and he avoided looking at either Raya or Manning.

Manning translated. Raya raised her eyes and looked at Proctor-Gould without saying anything. She seemed to be studying him, and she looked as if she were troubled by some thought remote from either of them.

'I want the suitcase,' repeated Proctor-Gould, still not looking at her.

She sighed and got to her feet.

'Let's go,' she said.

They went downstairs. Proctor-Gould's black Chaika was waiting at the kerb, and they got in. Raya gave an address to the driver, and the car moved off in a northerly direction, through Okhotniy Ryad into Sverdlov Square. Proctor-Gould stared out of the window expressionlessly. Raya sat on the jump-seat opposite him, watching his face, her forehead a little puckered as if she were puzzled by something.

23

They drove to a public dining-room, Dietary Dining-Room No. 37, in a forlorn street behind the White Russia Station. Outside, the stucco was flaking. Inside, the room was as bleak as a prison, and the clattering of metal trays and the scrape of cutlery on plates echoed noisily between the bare walls. It was half past three; a dozen or so late lunchers or early diners were gulping down their dietary mush with all possible speed. The air was steamy, and heavy with sour smells.

They bought yoghourt and coffee in order to be allowed in, and then Raya led them across to a table in the corner. There was a young man wearing steel-framed spectacles sitting at the table, with a number of empty coffee cups in front of him. He got to his feet as they approached. Without looking at Raya he took the tray from Manning and set it down. Then he gravely shook the two men's hands. He did not seem surprised to see them.

'This is Konstantin,' said Raya.

'Pleased to meet you,' said Konstantin in Russian, as they all sat down. He neither got nor asked for the other half of the introduction.

Manning guessed that Konstantin was somewhere in his late twenties. He seemed surprisingly shabby for a black-market speculator. His jacket was slightly too small for him, exposing soiled shirt-cuffs and three or four inches of scrawny wrist. The lapels of the jacket were permanently cockled, and the tie, tied crooked in a collar which was loose about his neck, had become neutral in colour with age and dirt. He looked quite unlike any of the elegant young men who came up to Manning in the street from time to time and offered to buy his clothes or his foreign currency.

His face fitted no better than his suit. It was pallid and

anxious, with a high, bony forehead. The lenses of his spectacles were thick, and seemed to slope backwards. Behind them his short-sighted eyes lurked magnified and ambiguous. Every now and then he impatiently pushed the bridge of the spectacles closer to his nose, and as they all sat for a long moment in silence he played with a coffee-spoon, beating it rapidly against the palm of his hand, and making as if to snap it in two.

Manning glanced at Proctor-Gould for instructions. Proctor-Gould looked tired, as if he had compressed a whole week's emotional energy into that one burst of anger.

'Does he speak English?' he asked Manning. 'No? You'd better do all the talking, then.'

Manning turned to Konstantin.

'An unfortunate mistake has occurred,' he began. 'Raya has disposed of some English books belonging to my friend here, not realizing that he wanted to keep them.'

Konstantin nodded.

'It was a silly misunderstanding,' said Manning. 'My friend, of course, is anxious to get them back.'

Konstantin nodded again.

'They were in a suitcase, a locked suitcase. I wonder if you've seen them?'

'Yes,' said Konstantin, nodding rapidly, almost impatiently.

'You acquired them from Raya?'

'Yes, yes, yes,' said Konstantin. Manning waited for him to go on, but Konstantin appeared not to think that any explanation was called for. He shook the coffee-spoon between his fingers as if it were a castanet, until it fell with a clatter into one of the empty cups.

'Well,' said Manning. 'we want the books back.'

Konstantin's eyes swam inscrutably behind his lenses.

'Have you any proof of ownership?' he asked, throwing the words away with such rapidity and diffidence that Manning did not at first catch them among the noise of the dining-room. 'Any documents? A receipt? A customs certificate?'

The question took Manning by surprise. He consulted with Proctor-Gould, who shook his head, staring at Konstantin curiously.

'All right,' said Konstantin, shrugging. 'Would you be prepared to come round to the militia-post and make a formal complaint?'

Again Manning consulted with Proctor-Gould.

'He says he wouldn't,' Manning translated to Konstantin, 'because he doesn't want to involve Raya.'

'I see,' said Konstantin.

'Anyway, the question is academic. You could scarcely go to the militia yourself, since you'd be charged with receiving.'

'Not if the books weren't stolen.'

'It doesn't make much difference. It's a criminal offence to buy or sell second-hand goods except through the State Commission Shops.'

'True,' said Konstantin. He smiled slightly. 'So the position is, we are unable to establish to whom the books belonged.'

'Just ask Raya where she got them from.'

'If Raya did steal them, she'd be a thief. I don't see why I should take the word of a thief.'

There was a silence. Again Konstantin shook the coffee-spoon, and again it fell into the cup.

'Suppose we abandon these barren theoretical speculations about ownership,' he said suddenly. 'Let's see if we can be practical. Now, why don't I treat you like any other potential customers, and offer to *sell* you the books?'

Manning translated this to Proctor-Gould. For a start Proctor-Gould said nothing. Then he sighed, and pulled at his ear.

'How much?' he said.

Manning was astonished that he should have accepted

the principle of this arrangement, and began to protest. Proctor-Gould cut him short.

'Ask him how much. We've nothing to lose by finding out what figure he has in mind.'

Manning asked him. Konstantin held up three fingers.

'Three hundred,' he said.

'Old roubles?'

'New roubles.'

Manning started to laugh.

'We're in the antiquarian market,' he told Proctor-Gould. 'He wants 300 roubles.'

Proctor-Gould frowned.

'How much is that in sterling? About £120?'

'Thereabouts, at the official rate. What was the cost of the books new?'

'I don't know. Twenty or thirty pounds at a guess. But they'd be worth more on the second-hand market in Moscow.'

'Nothing like £120, Gordon. Particularly since they're stolen.'

'I suppose not.'

Proctor-Gould had bent close to the table, scraping it with the prong of a fork.

'What shall I say, then, Gordon?'

'Offer him 200 roubles.'

Manning stared at Proctor-Gould in surprise.

'I can't understand you, Gordon,' he said. 'I don't see why you should pay anything at all. But to pay more than the books were worth in the first place . . . !'

'I think that's my affair, Paul.'

'Look, Gordon, you've got this business out of all proportion. . . .'

'Some of those books aren't mine, Paul. They belong to my clients. Now, offer him 200 roubles.'

Manning hesitated. Konstantin and Raya watched the two Englishmen. Manning felt their eyes shift back and forth from him to Proctor-Gould, trying to read the sense of their dispute.

'All right,' he said to Konstantin at last. 'My friend will give you 200 roubles. But only because he is acting on ...'

'Two hundred and eighty,' interrupted Konstantin, throwing off the figure like a verbal shrug.

Proctor-Gould reflected when Manning told him. Then he opened his eyes very wide, blinked several times, and opened them wide again. He seemed to be fighting off sleep.

'Two hundred and fifty,' he said. 'And that really is the highest I'll go.'

Konstantin accepted the figure at once, with a little twist of the head and a wry tightening of the mouth, as if admitting the truth of some unwelcome proposition.

'It's low,' he said. 'Your friend would go higher if I pushed him. But why bother? If I had the books I'd accept 250 for them.'

Manning stared at him.

'What do you mean, *if* you had the books?'

'I mean,' said Konstantin with casual rapidity, 'given that, in the circumstances that, it being the case that ...'

'You haven't actually got them?'

'No, I've sold them already.'

Manning was so surprised that for a moment he was unable even to translate the announcement. When he did, Proctor-Gould raised his head and gazed at Konstantin in silence. The inspection disconcerted Konstantin. He blinked, and twitched, and shifted in his seat. Again he dropped the spoon into his cup.

'Look,' he said suddenly. 'I know how attached one can get to certain books. Perhaps I could come to some arrangements with the buyer. Would that interest you?'

'How much would it cost?' asked Manning.

'Well, listen. I don't think he'd let us have the lot back. Judging by what he said at the time. But he might agree to part with one, if I explained the circumstances. If you'd

108

like to tell me what one you want most, I could have a try.'

Proctor-Gould stared at him, his great brown eyes wide open and unblinking, his face completely expressionless, not even turning his head when Manning translated.

'How much?' he asked.

'Provided it's only one,' said Konstantin slowly, 'you can have it for nothing.'

Proctor-Gould stared and stared, not answering. Then, abruptly, he got to his feet.

'Let's go,' he said to Manning.

Konstantin sat back in his chair and gazed up at Proctor-Gould.

'You don't want it?' he asked. 'Not even for nothing?'

'Come on,' said Proctor-Gould to Manning.

'One minute,' said Konstantin. He tore a page out of a note-book, scribbled something on it in ballpoint, and gave it to Manning.

'In case your friend changes his mind,' he said.

Outside the Chaika was still waiting.

'What shall I tell the driver?' asked Manning, as they got in.

Proctor-Gould didn't reply. He sat gazing out of the window, pulling at his ear.

'What's on that piece of paper he gave you?' he asked suddenly.

'An address: "Churavayev к.s., Kurumalinskaya Street 93, Flat 67".'

'Konstantin's?'

'I suppose so.'

'Give the name of the street to the driver. Tell him to drop us on the corner.'

As the car pulled away Manning became aware of a face looking in from the pavement. It was Raya. She seemed uncertain, as if she was unable to make up her mind whether to rap on the window, and when Manning looked back as the car turned the corner at the end of the street, she was still standing there, gazing uncertainly after them.

24

Kurumalinskaya Street turned out to be familiar. It was one of the narrow, busy thoroughfares Manning had walked along with Katerina, talking of God and love. Number 93 was a seedy tenement block lined on the street side with small, flyblown shops. The entrance gateway lay between a sign saying FO TWE R REPAI S and a grocery. The window of the grocery was boarded up, and on the boards someone had whitewashed: 'Overfulfill the plan for the distributive sector!' The letters had dribbled down to the pavement and had the appearance of being on stalks, as if they were an organic product of dereliction, a sort of complex urban cow-parsley growing out of the grey pavement.

'I still don't see what we're going to do,' said Manning, as they gazed at the outside.

'We're going to take advantage of Konstantin's mistake,' said Proctor-Gould. His weariness had vanished. He seemed excited.

'What mistake?'

'He shouldn't have given us his address, Paul.'

'Why not? He had to, if you were ever going to take up his offer.'

'He should have rung later.'

'What's the difference?'

They walked through the archway into the courtyard. It was full of noise and movement. Small children ran about without apparent direction, shouting. An old woman walked painfully from one doorway to another with a bucket of water. A man with a shaven head wearing striped pyjamas came out of a door, walked slowly into the middle of the yard, stopped, yawned, scratched each armpit in turn, and then walked slowly back again.

'The difference,' said Proctor-Gould, as they cast about for the right staircase, 'is that we're going to get all the books back. For nothing.'

'But how can we? Konstantin isn't at home now.'

'Exactly, Paul.'

'You're not thinking of breaking in, Gordon?'

'We'll see.'

'But the books aren't there. Konstantin sold them.'

'I don't think he did, Paul. I don't think he can have done. Look, he was already back in the restaurant waiting for Raya to bring the second case when we arrived, and he'd had time to drink at least three cups of coffee. In fact he must have been expecting Raya about three-quarters of an hour earlier – at the time she would have arrived if I hadn't stopped her. In other words, the only time he had to dispose of the first case was about as long as it would take Raya to get to the hotel and return with the second one. How long would that be? Well, it depends whether she went by bus or took a taxi. Either way it can't have been much more than half an hour. Now I don't believe that within half an hour he can have got the case open, examined the books, and found a buyer for them.'

'You think he just took the case home and dumped it?'

'Wouldn't you, if you'd been in his position?'

'I suppose so.'

A small boy crashed into Manning's legs, looked up at the two abstracted faces above him, and ran away shouting.

'But, Gordon,' said Manning, 'why did Konstantin say he'd sold the books if he hadn't?'

'I don't know. Perhaps as an excuse for raising the price by claiming that he had to cover the fence's margin as well.'

'But that's not the line he took at all. He said that he couldn't get all the books back at any price. And then he said that he could get any one of them back for nothing.'

Proctor-Gould stopped and gazed at the ground, pulling his ear. Some of the children stood round in a semi-circle, watching them, and an old woman sitting on a doorstep shouted something that Manning couldn't catch.

'Well, I don't know,' said Proctor-Gould finally. 'It was some piece of sales talk. The details aren't important. All I'm interested in is getting the books back. Come on.'

Manning followed Proctor-Gould dubiously up a staircase in the corner of the yard. The walls of the staircase were pitted all over, as if they had been subjected to rifle fire, worn down to such a variety of levels of paint and plaster and brick that the mottling seemed almost uniform and intentional. On each dark landing there were four front doors, all of them the colour of Konstantin's tie – neutral with age and dirt – except at the edges and around the locks, where use had exposed the wood itself.

The front door of number 67 was exactly like the rest, identified only by a rusted and empty bell-push on the lintel, with a piece of card stuffed behind the flange bearing the name 'Churavayev' in a ballpoint scribble.

Proctor-Gould rapped on the door with his knuckles.

'Gordon, what am I going to say . . . ?' began Manning.

'Sh!'

They listened. There was no sound from the other side of the door. Proctor-Gould knocked again. Then he kicked, making the heavy door reverberate in its frame. At this the next door but one opened a crack, revealing an inch of pyjama and a sleepy eye.

'They're not in,' said the man, apparently trying not to wake himself up any further by the effort of opening or closing his mouth. 'So shove off.'

'Thanks,' said Manning, as the door shut again. He passed the message on to Proctor-Gould. Proctor-Gould leaned his weight against the door of 67 and pushed.

'Don't be a fool,' said Manning.

Proctor-Gould went on pushing, grunting a little, scarcely breathing, until his face was visibly dark even in the darkness of the landing.

'For Christ's sake, Gordon,' said Manning, looking round to see if anyone could see them.

Proctor-Gould stopped pushing and got his breath back. Then he stepped back to the other side of the landing, bunched his right shoulder up, and charged at the door, changing his mind at the last moment and waltzing round so that he stopped himself awkwardly against the door with the flat of his hands and his forehead.

'I think perhaps not,' he said, rubbing his head. He took his key-ring out of his pocket and tried all the possible-looking keys on it.

'Gordon, it's not worth risking it just for the sake of a few books.'

Proctor-Gould put the keys away and took out a tiny pearl-handled penknife, with which he began to prod about in the keyhole. Then, abruptly, he straightened up.

'Did you say the man said *they*, plural, were out?' he asked.

'I think that's what he said.'

Proctor-Gould began to peer closely at the lintel, running his hands over the pock-marked wood. Then he gazed about the landing walls.

'Now what are you up to?' asked Manning, becoming more indulgent now that it was clear nothing embarrassing was going to occur after all.

'If there's more than one person living here they may have left a communal key hidden outside somewhere.'

He got down on his hands and knees and crawled about the filthy landing, testing the skirting-board and the risers of the stairs. Manning began to laugh.

'I must say, Gordon,' he said, 'this display of determination is a new side to your character.'

Proctor-Gould put his face nearer and nearer to the floor,

until at last he was squinting along it, with his cheek resting on it.

'If anyone comes by,' said Manning, 'I'll tell them you're a Moslem. Your face will certainly be dusky enough.'

Proctor-Gould was quite still.

'I can see it,' he said. 'It's under the door.'

He crawled across to the door, and ran his hand along the floor in front of it.

'On a thread,' he added, finding it, and pulling it until the key slid out. He stood up, and without even stopping to brush the dust off his face and knees, unlocked the door and walked inside.

Manning stayed where he was.

'Come on,' said Proctor-Gould. 'Don't let's stand here with the door open.'

'I don't want to have anything to do with this . . .' began Manning, but he stopped. Someone was coming out of an apartment on the floor above. They both listened. There was the sound of a front door shutting, and of a key being turned in a lock. Then the noise of footsteps descending the stairs. One, two, three . . . in another six or seven steps the man would reach the semi-landing, turn, and look down on them as they stood, half in and half out of the apartment. Manning stepped inside and shut the door. At once Proctor-Gould locked it behind them.

'Now,' he said, 'the sooner we find the books the sooner we can go.'

25

There was only one room in the apartment. It was about twelve feet wide by fifteen feet long, and it looked out not on the courtyard but a derelict back-street running behind the block, lined with shuttered single-storey buildings which sagged in the middle, and plots of waste land covered with old boxes and rusty oil drums. Against one wall of the room was an unmade bed; in the corner, a primus stove standing on an asbestos sheet, and a dirty frying-pan; under the window a solid mahogany desk, covered with a confusion of books, papers, pencils, protractors and luxuriant pot plants.

There was scarcely any wall to be seen. Almost every inch of it was covered with books, crammed on to thin makeshift shelves which sagged under the weight, giving the room an odd impression of being hung with swagged draperies. On the shelves in front of the books was a confusion of objects for which there was no room anywhere else – framed photographs of people in the fashions of thirty years before, pen-and-ink sketches, a marble bust of Lomonosov, a compass, a cheap icon, a jar of feathers, pebbles, birds' eggs, pieces of quartz, dried flowers, solid projections of mathematical functions, a metronome, a gramophone with a home-made amplifier and a dusty stack of long-playing records without envelopes. It was a dark, overstuffed, sympathetic room, a young man's room that had gone to seed. The air smelt of frying and paraffin and sleeping.

Manning picked up a single nylon stocking which was lying across the back of a chair.

'Wife? Girl friend?' he said, showing it to Proctor-Gould.

Proctor-Gould threw back the bedclothes to look under the bed. It revealed an assortment of women's shoes, all well-worn, standing in a silent grey desert of dust.

'She doesn't seem to have done much housework recently,' he said.

Manning sat down at the desk, on an ancient swivel-chair with stuffing leaking out of its torn upholstery. There were crumbs among the papers on the desk, and a plate covered with cold grey grease. There was also a mirror on a swivel stand. Manning adjusted it slightly so that he could see himself. What on earth did Konstantin want a mirror on his desk for? It was difficult to believe from his appearance that he had ever examined his reflection in his life. But of course, it was for the woman; the desk/dining-table was also her dressing-table. He lifted some papers, and found a lipstick without a top, a broken eyebrow pencil, and a small jar of cold cream.

He tried to imagine Konstantin's woman sitting there, among all the books and the masculine curiosities. Were some of the books and papers hers? Did she work at the desk, too, and own a share of the room's character? Or was she indifferent to it, creating a small life in the midst of it all with her own props – the shoes, the cold cream, the broken eyebrow pencil? He pictured them getting up in the morning. He saw Konstantin, not her, putting the coffee on the primus. She would be sitting in the swivel-chair in her underwear, gazing at herself expressionlessly in the mirror, rubbing cream into her skin. She was self-contained, indifferent to him. If he asked her a question, she would let a minute go by before she answered. There was total confusion in the room; her clothes were scattered everywhere.

But somehow the room didn't quite fit the picture. There should have been more confusion, more traces of her. A stocking, a few pairs of shoes – why were there no dresses lying around? Why was there no underwear hanging up to dry? One lipstick, one jar of cold cream, one eyebrow pencil – why was the eyebrow pencil broken?

He looked closely at the cold cream jar. It was covered in a fine film of dust. It hadn't been opened for – how long? A week? Two weeks? A month? How quickly did dust collect in Moscow? He went across to the bed. There was a pair of men's pyjamas mixed up in the bedding. But no nightdress. Nothing to indicate that a woman had slept there.

'I think she's left him,' he said.

Proctor-Gould was searching among some clothes crammed behind a dusty curtain in the corner.

'She expects to come back, then,' he said. 'She's left some of her clothes on the rail here. Look at this.'

He held up a pale blue evening dress, with silk flounces and sequins. The colour had faded – the silk was almost brown in places – and a number of sequins were missing.

'Rather a museum piece, isn't it?' he said, giggling. 'Konstantin must have a pretty curious taste in lady friends.'

But the sight of the dress softened Manning towards the girl.

'I expect her parents bought her that when she was about seventeen,' he said. 'It's rather touching she should have kept it. Incidentally, they must have moved in exalted circles. There aren't many places in Moscow where you wear long evening gowns.'

Proctor-Gould hung the dress up again.

'Perhaps they quarrelled,' said Manning, 'and she walked out without having time to pack everything.'

Proctor-Gould shrugged.

'She's probably gone off on some sort of business trip,' he said. 'Or living with someone else for a month. Some of these Soviet girls are pretty casual, you know. But never mind her – where's the suitcase?'

Manning went slowly along the bookshelves, running his eye along the titles. There were all the standard Russian classics, and a number of foreign ones in translation. Farther on there were shelves full of books on Russian history and Russian economic geography, then a row of textbooks on mechanics, mathematics, and aircraft construction, tables of engineering constants, and forty or fifty issues of a learned journal devoted to high-temperature metallurgy.

Manning was surprised to find a number of philosophical works in French and German, expounding existentialism and positivism. At random he took down Carnap's *Der logische Aufbau der Welt*. There was a tram ticket between pages nine and ten. Before the ticket the margins were full of scribbled translations of even quite simple words. After the ticket they were empty. On another shelf were books about the Soviet Union written by foreigners who had visited it. Manning noticed Gide's *Retour de l'URSS*. The margins were full of translation notes all the way through. He wondered how much it had cost Konstantin on the black market.

'Well?' said Proctor-Gould.

'No luck so far.'

He went on looking; it upset and offended him to think that this intelligent and coherent library had been assembled by a petty criminal. Perhaps it was all stolen property.

Among a small selection of books on Borodin and Glinka he came across a copy of *A Hero of Our Time*. An odd place for it to be – particularly since there was another copy of it among the rest of Lermontov's works. It occurred to him that he had passed two separate copies of *An Economic History of the R.S.F.S.R.* in different places. A moment later he saw *The Behaviour of Aerofoils in Lateral Turbulence* for the second time round, and two copies of *The Nimzovich Defence*.

Puzzled, he stared at the spines of the two *Nimzovich Defences*. They seemed to be the same edition. The only difference between them was that one was in a dust-jacket and one was not. He looked back to the two copies of *The Behaviour of Aerofoils*. Again, they were the same edition. Again, the only difference was that one was dust-jacketed and one was not.

He saw the explanation suddenly and completely, as if it had been held up on a card in front of him. He took out the copy of *The Behaviour of Aerofoils* with the dust-jacket and opened it. Inside the jacket was a copy of Yeats's *Collected Poems*.

'One of yours?' asked Manning.

'Ah!' said Proctor-Gould.

They began to pull out all the other dust-jacketed books they could see on the shelves one after another, throwing them down on the floor if the jackets did not conceal volumes belonging to Proctor-Gould, until they had recovered some twenty books.

'I wonder where the suitcase is?' said Manning.

'Somewhere on that waste lot outside the window, I should think.'

'Any more to come?' asked Manning. 'I think it's about time we left.'

'There should be one or two. What's that one you've got there?'

It was the *Proceedings of the Institute of Civic Studies*. Proctor-Gould took it out of Manning's hands and flicked through it.

'All right,' he said. 'Let's call it a day.'

'Just a moment,' said Manning. He put his hand into the gap left by the *Proceedings* and pulled out something which had been concealed behind the row of books. It was a tin of Nescafé.

They both stared at it without a word. Then Manning pulled out all the other books on the shelf. There, lined up against the wall at the back, were four more tins of Nescafé.

'You lost six, didn't you?' asked Manning.

'She brought one back.'

They picked up the tins and examined them. One of them was almost empty, as it had been when it disappeared from Proctor-Gould's room. The others were still full. But they had all been opened and unsealed.

'What do you make of it?' asked Manning.

Proctor-Gould shrugged.

'I suppose he opened them to make sure they were genuine.'

Manning thought.

'Would you have opened them,' he said, 'if you'd been buying them?'

'I might.'

'You wouldn't, Gordon. Not if you'd wanted to sell them again.'

'If I had a suspicious nature . . .'

'You might have opened one at random as a sample, Gordon. But not all of them.'

Proctor-Gould fixed Manning with his great brown gaze.

'What's your explanation then?' he asked.

'I think he was looking for something.'

'Looking for something? What?'

'I don't know, Gordon. Do you?'

Proctor-Gould went on gazing at Manning for some moments. But the focus of his eyes shifted, so that he seemed to be looking right through Manning's head at the wall beyond. Finally a great sigh heaved his shoulders up and dropped them again.

'No, Paul,' he said. 'No, I don't.'

There was a conclusion about another matter that the tins suggested to Manning. He caught Proctor-Gould's eye.

'I wonder if you're thinking what I'm thinking,' he said.

'What about, Paul?'

'Who the girl is who shares Konstantin's room.'

'Oh, that,' said Proctor-Gould. He sighed again. 'Yes, that did occur to me.'

'No mystery about her any longer.'

'No.'

'Nor where she's been for the past few weeks.'

'I suppose not.'

Proctor-Gould picked up the single nylon stocking and rubbed it softly between finger and thumb, then put it in his pocket. He noticed Manning watching him.

'She's probably looking for it,' he said.

26

They staggered along Kurumalinskaya Street with their arms full of books until they found a taxi, and drove to one of the big department stores, where they bought another suitcase to put the books in. Then they took the bus to the Kiev Station, and deposited the suitcase in the left luggage office.

'Will you keep the ticket, Paul?' asked Proctor-Gould. 'Now that we've got things straight again I don't want to take any more chances.'

When Manning had folded the ticket away in his wallet he looked up and found that Proctor-Gould was gazing at him, his head a little on one side, so that he could just touch the lobe of his ear with the tip of his finger.

'It's a strange business,' said Proctor-Gould.

'Yes.'

Proctor-Gould went on looking at Manning.

'You were very quiet on the bus, Paul,' he said. 'It occurred to me that these events might be imposing some strain on the confidence between us. I suppose they might suggest that I'm involved in some undertaking outside my work for my clients.'

Manning was silent.

'I see that, Paul,' said Proctor-Gould. 'It certainly does seem as if Konstantin was looking for something in those Nescafé tins. But on my honour, Paul, I've no idea what.'

Manning still said nothing. They began to pace slowly across the station, side by side. It was a good place for confidential talk, thought Manning. They looked as if they were waiting for a train.

'Then again,' said Proctor-Gould, 'the business of the books seems even odder. Why did Konstantin say he'd sold them when they were in his room all the time? Was it just to get me to raise my offer? But then he said he couldn't get them all back at any price – only one of them for nothing. Another explanation struck me when we saw his room. He's an educated man – perhaps he wanted the books simply for his own use. But in that case, why did he make me a price in the first place? What do you think, Paul?'

'I don't know, Gordon.'

'I know what was worrying you, Paul. You thought I was prepared to pay rather a lot to get the books back. I can only say what I said before. A lot of those books don't belong to me. I may be old-fashioned, but if someone entrusts me with something I feel a certain obligation to take care of it. And since I'd lost these books – through my own foolishness, as I fully recognize – I felt obliged to make considerable sacrifices to get them back. I don't think there's anything mysterious about that.'

Manning drew in breath to reply, then let it out again.

'In fact, Paul,' said Proctor-Gould, 'two hundred roubles here or there really doesn't mean very much in terms of what it costs me to stay in Russia anyway. I should have charged it to expenses, of course. It was a much bigger sacrifice to break into Konstantin's room, I can tell you. I've never deliberately put myself on the wrong side of the law before. I shan't be doing it again, either.'

They turned at the far side of the station, and began to walk back.

'I think *my* motives in all this are fairly clear,' said Proctor-Gould. 'What Konstantin's are I don't know. It looks as if he thought there was one book I should value above all the rest, and he wanted to find out which. Why did he think it would be valuable to me? It couldn't be anything about the book as a book. None of them has any value to a collector. None of them is on the banned list in Russia – I took great care about that. It would have to be something the book contained. Now if we rule out secret compartments and the like, there's nothing much a book can contain, except perhaps some sort of message. Perhaps something in code, perhaps in one of those micro-dots one reads about. In other words, it looks as if Konstantin was trying to blackmail me because he thought I was involved in some sort of espionage.'

'It's possible,' said Manning.

'Not that it's really necessary to follow Konstantin's reasoning through. You'd reached the same conclusion about me yourself, hadn't you, Paul?'

'Well, look, Gordon. . . .'

'I'm not complaining, Paul. I'm rather flattered to be taken for a spy. It just doesn't happen to be the case.'

'I must admit, Gordon, the thought occurred to me. It seemed a logical explanation of the facts. But as a matter of fact I'd rejected it.'

Proctor-Gould looked at Manning with interest. As they paced along Manning could feel the great brown eyes examining his profile, as if the shape of his nose or the configurations of his ear might hold some clue to the thoughts taking place inside.

'I've come to know you quite well in the past few weeks,' said Manning. 'At first I thought you were rather a charlatan. All this interest in improving Anglo-Soviet relations – I thought it was just a way of making more money and more contacts. But now I don't think it is. You're a public man, Gordon. You don't do things for complex or ambiguous reasons, like the rest of us. You do simple things with simple aims for simple motives. People always suspect that public men are dishonest and insincere. But from observing you, Gordon, I don't think they can be. Dishonesty and insincerity are too complex to be within the range of public men. Public men may deceive others – but only if they are deceiving themselves, too. They're part of their own audience. I don't think you could promote good relations between Britain and Russia with one hand, and undermine them with the other. I don't think your character is capable of such complexity.'

Proctor-Gould thought about this for some moments.

'Thank you, Paul,' he said at last. 'I must admit, I'm rather touched. It's the testimonial I should most have liked to hear about myself.'

'Not a testimonial, Gordon – a dispassionate observation.'

'All the more pleasing, Paul.'

He stopped, and gazed intently at Manning, pulling his ear.

'Look, Paul,' he said. 'I appreciate your confidence in me. I appreciate it very deeply indeed. Let me in return be absolutely frank and categoric. Konstantin and Raya may believe I have something incriminating in my possession. They may even be right; it's possible that I have such a thing. But if I have, what it is and how I came by it I know no more than you.'

Manning nodded.

'I give you my word on that, Paul,' said Proctor-Gould.

'As an Englishman?' asked Manning humorously.

'As a Johnsman, if you like.'

27

'I've made up my mind about Raya,' said Proctor-Gould suddenly, as they sat in a taxi on the way back to the National. 'I'm going to give her her marching orders. I don't know whether that relieves your mind at all?'

'It certainly helps,' said Manning. 'You're striking her off your list of clients, too?'

'I'm afraid so. As soon as we get back to the hotel I'm going to ask her to leave. Or perhaps I should say, ask you to ask her to leave.'

'You could put it like that.'

'Don't worry, Paul, I shan't start a scene. Or rather, we shan't.'

'Shan't we?'

'No, I think we should be quite firm, but at the same time perfectly polite and level-headed. It won't be particularly agreeable while it lasts, I admit. But it's just one of those unpleasant necessities that crop up from time to time. We shall just have to grin and bear it, Paul.'

'I see.'

'By dinner-time it will all be over and done with. We shall be laughing about it.'

But by the time the taxi pulled up outside the hotel Proctor-Gould's resolution had ebbed. He began to climb out, then got back in and sat down again beside Manning.

'Do you suppose Raya's up there at the moment?' he asked.

'I don't know, Gordon.'

'I was just wondering whether she'd be waiting for us, or whether we'd have to sit down and wait for her. I'm just trying to get the situation clear in my own mind, you see.'

'She'll be in the bath, I expect.'

'In the bath? I hadn't thought of that, Paul.'

He pulled at his ear, and gazed gloomily at the visible mid-parts of the commissionaire who was standing holding the car door open, as if trying to divine the contents of the man's stomach.

'I suppose she will,' he said reluctantly. 'That possibility hadn't occurred to me, I must admit.'

'I was joking, Gordon. . . .'

'No, no. It's getting on for six. That's where she'll be, all right. Look, Paul, I wonder if the best arrangement wouldn't be this. I'll wait down here in the taxi while you go up and tell her what we've decided.'

'For God's sake, Gordon! I can't just stand there and shout through the bathroom door that you're chucking her out.'

'I appreciate the difficulty, Paul. But let's face facts. It wouldn't make things any easier for you if I was standing out there with you, would it?'

'But Gordon, you could go *into* the bathroom.'

'I could go in – but I couldn't say anything. You'd still have to stand outside shouting a translation.'

He pulled at his ear in silence again.

'Anyway,' he said, 'I don't know that I could go in, could I? I mean, I'm not sure that it's quite the done thing to look at a girl in the bath while you're telling her that it's all over between you.'

'Aren't you being a shade hypersensitive, Gordon?'

'I don't think so. In fact, I think one might make out a better case for doing it the other way round – my staying outside while you go in. After all, you were a great pal of hers at one stage.'

'Not as great as all that. We've been into this before, Gordon.'

'All the same, she's a perfectly unconventional sort of girl. I'm sure she wouldn't stand on ceremony.'

They sat in silence for a moment or two, while the commissionaire bent down and examined them through the door, trying to remember whether he was seeing them in or seeing them out.

'No?' said Proctor-Gould. 'Well, I wonder, Paul, if it wouldn't be better to let things run on for the time being, and try to find a more suitable moment to break it to her in the next few days?'

'I don't think that would be a good idea at all, Gordon.'

'All right, then. Supposing I just quietly took a room in another hotel, and waited for it all to blow over?'

'No, Gordon.'

'Well, let's leave it like this. We'll creep in quietly, and if she *is* in the bath, we'll just creep quietly out again and wait till she emerges.'

28

But Raya was not in the bath, nor in the room. She had gone, and she had taken all her belongings with her. The pictures on the wall – the pyjamas under the pillow – the stockings and underclothes in the bathroom; they had all vanished. Apart from some wilting birch twigs in a vase, the room had returned to the gloom in which Manning had first seen it.

The two men walked vaguely about, touching things, unable to get used to the idea.

'Well,' said Proctor-Gould, 'I suppose one ought to be grateful.'

'I suppose at any rate we might have guessed.'

'The room looks so strange. It takes a bit of getting used to.'

He looked disconsolately about. Then he remembered something, and took out of his pocket the single stocking they had found at Konstantin's. He looked at it for a moment, then tossed it on to the chest of drawers. It landed half on and half off, and poured itself slowly over the edge on to the floor, where it remained, unnoticed by Proctor-Gould, in a sad little heap.

'Anyway,' he said, 'let's have some Nescafé.'

He fetched the little kettleful of water, opened one of the tins they had recovered, and went through the familiar, soothing ritual.

'Ah, Paul,' he said, taking up his old position in front of the radiator, and stirring the brown fluid with the same old apostle spoon. 'She led me a terrible dance. Of course, it was my fault. I made a fool of myself. I appreciate that now.'

'These things happen, Gordon.'

'Sometimes she wouldn't even look at me for a whole day. She'd just lie on the bed there, reading or smoking, and not pay the slightest attention to me. I didn't know what to do with myself. I think they were the most awful days of my life.'

'I know what you mean.'

'Then sometimes she could be so sweet! I don't know how to explain exactly. She'd do little things for me – iron a shirt, or suddenly bring me a cup of Nescafé. I can't really explain.'

He had difficulty with his voice. It wavered a little, and he coughed, and fell silent, and coughed again.

'No, I know what you mean,' said Manning.

'I mean, I'd feel we were really making contact. I'd talk to her, Paul.'

'What – in English?'

'I know it sounds silly. I used to tell her about England. Sometimes I'd describe my parents' house, where I was brought up. It's in Norwood. Do you know Norwood at all?'

'Not really. But do you think Raya understood any of this?'

Proctor-Gould sighed and pulled at his ear, gazing reflectively into the corner of the room.

'Well, I occasionally had the feeling that she more or less knew what I was driving at. She used to talk as well sometimes. We used to have quite long conversations.'

'Did you understand what she said at all?'

'Well, you know how it is, Paul. I had a general sense that we were getting through to each other. Does that sound absurd?'

'No, no.'

'I don't want to underestimate your services as an interpreter, Paul. But sometimes I think we achieved a sort of telepathic communication that didn't really depend on the actual spoken words at all. That's what I felt at the time, anyway.'

'And then she'd pinch something?'

Proctor-Gould sighed again.

'I suppose I made rather a fool of myself,' he said sadly. Manning was moved.

'I suppose I did, too, Gordon,' he said.

'You could talk to her, of course.'

'Yes, I suppose I could talk to her.'

They sat in silence for some moments, thinking about her.

'The first time we met,' said Manning in a faraway voice, not looking at Proctor-Gould, 'was on a sort of picnic in the forest near Maliye Zemyati.'

'I know. I was there, Paul.'

'The sun was shining. But it was quite cold – there was still snow lying in places.'

'I remember.'

'We just walked through the woods. And climbed trees. I suppose it sounds a bit pastoral.'

'No, I know what you mean.'

'We came to this lake. There was this kind of wooden landing stage thing. We lay down on it in the sunshine, side by side. Everything seemed somehow so simple and uncomplicated – I can't explain.'

He fell silent, gazing into the depths of the escritoire. Proctor-Gould watched him. Neither of them moved.

'After a while,' said Manning, 'she said we should take our clothes off.'

There was another long silence. It scarcely seemed that either of them was breathing.

'And go for a swim in the lake,' said Manning at last. Proctor-Gould opened his eyes very wide.

'And go for a swim in the lake?' he queried. 'With *snow* on the ground?'

He began to giggle his silly girlish giggle. For a moment Manning felt himself blushing. Then he began to laugh, too.

'Of course, we *didn't*,' he explained above the strange contralto whinnying coming from Proctor-Gould. Somehow the explanation struck them both as being even more ridiculous than the original proposal, and they began to laugh all over again.

Eventually their laughter ebbed, and they became serious.

'Did you ever, in point of fact,' said Proctor-Gould, 'enjoy her favours, as I believe they call it?'

'No – I've told you before. Did you?'

'No.'

'I suspected not.'

'I suppose she is what rather vulgar people at Cambridge used to call a prick-teaser.'

'I suppose she is.'

They both sighed, and became companionably silent.

'Anyway,' said Proctor-Gould, 'she did know when to go. And she did leave in a very quiet and decent manner.'

'Yes,' said Manning.

A thought struck him.

'I suppose she didn't by any chance take the *second* case of books with her when she went, did she?'

Proctor-Gould crossed the room in two strides and wrenched open the wardrobe.

She had.

29

'Do you understand it, Katya?' asked Manning.

'I don't want to understand it,' said Katerina. 'It's not worth understanding.'

It was late at night, and they were walking down a long, empty road somewhere on the outskirts. On both sides of the road, for as far as the eye could see, the scattered street-lamps shone weakly on tussocks of dusty grass and tall concrete fences. From behind the fences the sudden drenching scent of lilacs came and went.

'It's not something that matters,' said Katerina. 'I'm not even thinking about it.'

Manning had been telling her about the books. Now he wished he had not. She had scarcely listened, she was so miserable, cross-grained, and metaphysical. Apparently Kanysh had still not written. Manning felt tired – literally sick and tired. An ague of tiredness had set into his bones.

'Sorry,' he said. 'I shouldn't have bothered you with it.'

'No, you shouldn't,' said Katya. 'You shouldn't bother yourself with it, either. All you want to do is to discover the contingent causes of contingent states of affairs. What do they matter? If it's not one reason for these people behaving as they did it's another. What we ought to use our God-given faculties to discover is the nature of those things which are *not* contingent, which *could not* be otherwise.'

'Surely it's right for us to try to understand our fellow human beings?'

'You don't come to know people by knowing about them. I know you very well, Paul, without knowing anything at all about you. I don't want to find out what you've done in the past, or why you did it. That would be idle curiosity. The answers would be irrelevant to what you now are. They might even conceal you from me.'

'I don't see it like that, Katya.'

'I know. That evening we met Korolenko I could feel the questions you were burning to ask. How did Korolenko know my name? Which of us was telling the truth? What had happened to make me so frightened of him?'

'I didn't ask them, Katya.'

'Only out of consideration. You thought them. You shouldn't have been interested in such things. What happened in the past has nothing to do with what I am now. Don't you know that God washes out the past each evening, as if it had never been, and that we are born again each morning? What happened yesterday is just gossip, Paul, just empty gossip.'

Manning didn't reply. Katerina's habit of projecting aspects of the truth across the whole screen of the universe suddenly irritated him. Somewhere far away the siren of a train wailed, and there was a crash of shunted trucks. He longed to leave Moscow.

'I'm glad Raya has left you in peace, anyway,' said Katerina. 'She brought out the worst in you. Her friend Konstantin Churavayev is like you, incidentally.'

'You know him?'

'His world is bounded by what? who? when? where? He is addicted to information.'

'What else do you know about him?'

'Nothing. In any case, it's not important. Don't gossip.'

Somewhere behind them a shoe scraped on the uneven roadway. Manning turned round. There was a man silhouetted against one of the yellowy patches of lamplight about thirty yards away. He was walking quietly in the same direction as themselves – the only person in the whole silent length of the street.

'Stop a moment, Katya,' said Manning.

He listened. There was silence in the road behind them. The man had stopped, too.

'What is it?' said Katya.

They began to walk again. So did the man. Now that he was listening for them, Manning could hear his footsteps fairly distinctly. He was walking close up against the concrete fence, where the cushioning clumps of weedy grass were thickest. Manning waited until he guessed the man was near a street-lamp.

'Stop,' he said quietly to Katerina.

'Now what . . .?'

'Sh!'

Again the man had stopped. Manning could see him bending down and doing something to his shoe. The light fell on a cap and an overcoat with upturned collar.

They walked on.

'Are we being followed?' said Katerina in a low voice.

'It looks like it.'

Katerina sighed, and pressed a handkerchief to her mouth nervously. Manning realized she had begun to walk more quickly. He had to hurry to keep up with her.

'Now, don't be silly, Katya,' he said. 'It doesn't matter if anyone sees where we're going. We're not doing anything wrong.'

'Please hurry.'

'It's silly to panic, Katya. It makes it look as if we've got something to hide.'

She hurried along without replying. She had begun to catch her breath in little gasps. Manning could hear the footsteps of their shadow keeping pace with theirs. He scuffed grit and macadam; he had evidently moved out from the rough grass to make better speed.

'Katya!' said Manning.

'Please, Paul!'

'What does it matter?'

'I don't want them to see us together.'

'We're not worth anyone's attention, Katya.'

'They'll think I've been telling you about my troubles. They'll say I've been telling you lies.'

'Oh, Katya!'

'And God knows what you're mixed up in, with Proctor-Gould and his affairs. They'll ask me about it. I know they will. They asked me questions before. Asked and asked. I can't go through all that again.'

Katya was almost running. However much he hurried, Manning was always a step behind her. He tried to breathe without panting, as if panting were a confession of guilty haste.

The dark street turned, and they merged into a broad, well-lit suburban highway, bordered as far as the eye could see in either direction by grey apartment blocks in various stages of construction, standing as plain and bald as shoe boxes among the desolation of builders' waste. On two or three of the blocks in the distance there was the glare of arc-lights where a night shift was working. There was no one else about. A car went by at speed. Then there was silence.

They found a bus stop, and Manning persuaded Katerina to wait there while they caught their breath. He hoped their shadower would suppose they had been hurrying for a bus. Katerina was sobbing. Manning offered her his handkerchief.

'It's nothing,' she said, pushing it away. 'Nothing, nothing.'

Over her shoulder he could see the man in the overcoat. In the brighter light of the highway he had dropped back and stopped about a hundred yards away. He appeared to be studying one of the official notice-boards where small advertisements were exhibited.

After a while a bus did in fact appear, creeping towards them with unbelievable slowness out of the gigantic suburban emptiness.

'Get on this bus, Katya,' said Manning. 'I'll wait behind at the stop. It's me he's following, not you. You go straight home, and don't get in touch with me again until I tell you it's all right.'

He bundled her aboard like a helpless bag of washing.

'Good-bye, Katya,' he said, squeezing her hand. 'Don't worry.'

Katya said nothing. Manning saw her through the window as the bus drew away, fumbling with her purse in front of the conductor's desk, her lower lip still pressed tremblingly outwards and upwards to contain her distress.

30

For some minutes after the bus had gone Manning remained by the stop, uncertain what to do. The man in the overcoat had made no attempt to catch the bus. He was still examining the notice-board a hundred yards away, bending close to decipher the cramped handwriting of the cards. There were just the two of them in the great formal emptiness of the prospect.

Manning shivered. He began to walk slowly along the broad pavement beside the highway in the direction Katya's bus had gone, back towards the centre of the city. He looked out of the corner of his eye. Unhurriedly, as if reluctant to stop reading, the man in the overcoat was turning away from the notice-board and following him.

Manning had never been followed before, so far as he knew. When he had first arrived in Moscow he had expected it. On his way to meet people whom he felt might have been compromised by a foreign acquaintance he had taken pains to double back on himself, to jump in and out of underground trains at the last moment. It had quickly come to seem very silly.

Now that he knew he was being followed he couldn't think what to do about it at all. He felt self-conscious about each step. It was like having a load on his back that he couldn't put down, that made the distance to be walked along the highway seem interminable.

He looked discreetly behind him. The man was still there. Every now and then a car or a lorry would go by along the road, and in the silence that followed he could hear the footsteps, quiet, distinct, unhurried.

He tried to work out why he was being followed. Evidently the authorities were interested in Proctor-Gould's affairs. What conclusion would they have come to? They would presumably know what had taken place in

Proctor-Gould's room, and no doubt Proctor-Gould's chauffeur had reported the visits to the public dining-room and Kurumalinskaya Street. But had their bargaining in the dining-room been overheard? Had they been seen in Konstantin's apartment? What sort of reading of the events could it be that made *his* movements of interest?

He half-turned his head. The man was still there. No nearer. No farther away.

He felt lonely. His solitude was thrown into relief by being observed. How long had the man been following him? Had he been there even before he had met Katya? Had the man watched him as he looked at the stills outside the cinema on Vorontzovskaya Street and brushed the dandruff off his shoulders? As he stopped in the doorway on Chkalovskaya, took off his shoe, and hopped about while he struggled to push a nail down with a fifty-kopeck piece?

And what could he do with this passenger on his back? He could not visit anyone, because it would implicate them. He could not run, or hide, or try to shake the man off, because it would seem suspicious. He could only behave normally. Or rather, make gestures of normality – bold, unambiguous, theatrical gestures that signalled normality to a man a hundred yards away. He could do nothing but walk, not too slowly, not too fast, down this enormous highway, between the hugely-spaced grey blocks and their attendant tower cranes, then continue through more vast, empty boulevards and prospects, until he returned to the great rhetorical remoteness of the university, and his own tiny room, there to go through the gestures of falling into an untroubled sleep.

Two long black cars sped by, one after another, their engine notes mingling and gradually dying. Silence again. And the footsteps.

Why follow *him*? The unreasonableness of it appalled him. What could he do that would illuminate anything for them? Where could he lead them that it would interest them to be? What fragment of information could he be expected to provide?

Then he remembered the crumpled slip of paper in his wallet – the receipt for the suitcase at the Kiev Station. Could they possibly know about *that*?

For the first time, Manning felt frightened. It was an indefinite fear, of being small and vulnerable among large forces that were indifferent to him. He thought of being questioned in bare rooms by men who saw him as nothing but an information-bearing object, uninteresting in itself. He thought of living for a great part of his life among hard, alien surfaces and clanging doors, unloved, unesteemed. He could not go on with this charade when possibilities like that opened out from it. He could not pretend to behave normally. The fragile pretensions of normality were crushed under the weight of such threats.

A line of tall evergreen bushes bordered the pavement. Just in front of Manning there was a break in the bushes, where muddy wheelmarks across the footway led to a track disappearing into the darkness of the construction site beyond. Without premeditation Manning turned off on to the track, and as soon as he was hidden by the bushes, began to run.

His own behaviour instantly terrified him. Oh God, he thought, I've done a stupid thing. How can I undo it? Oh God, how can I undo it?

He looked about him as he ran. Dimly, in the light filtering through from the highway, he took in the paraphernalia of construction – a shed, a heap of wooden scaffolding, a trailer covered with a tarpaulin. He must hide. But where? Somewhere darker. He ran on. The side of a building loomed vaguely, with unglazed windows. A doorway without a door. Into it. Inside it was completely dark. His footsteps reverberated about the bare concrete walls. A smell of cement and damp. Stop panting! Quiet, quiet.

Silence. Oh, you fool, you *fool*! No, stop. Not even think. Press against wall. Try not to be.

Wait for the man.

Not a sound. What's he doing? Would have run to gap in bushes – must have reached it by now. Looking cautiously round corner?

What's happening? Why silence so long?

Suddenly, the footsteps – running. Coming along the track towards the building, louder and louder. Now outside the door!

Now stopped. Not five feet from the door. Can hear him panting. Can hear soles of shoes on the ground – shirrrrrr. Pause. Shirrrrrr. He's turning to look, first one way, then the other.

Then step, step, step – coming nearer. The echoing crunch of a step on the concrete floor of the doorway. He was inside the room. The whole room was suddenly full of his breathing, of the scurring of his shoes on the concrete. Oh God! Don't breathe! Don't even look at him! Keep face pressed against concrete wall! Just wait.

And wait.

He must be looking this way. The darkness dissolves in his presence. Any moment . . . any moment. . . .

Two decisive steps on the concrete, and quieter steps going away on the beaten earth outside. Silence.

Gone.

Breathe. Wait. Complete silence outside. Wait longer. Still silence. Now what?

What indeed?

Slip back to the highway? Then what? Run? Run down that endless road – run and run and run until the breath gave out? The hopeless futility of it appalled him. But what else was there to do? He had panicked. The consequences stretched before him like a progression of rooms in a dream, each opening inexorably off the last.

With infinite precaution he crept to the door and edged

his head slowly round the lintel. After the darkness inside the building, the dim light outside from the street-lamps on the highway seemed like day. He made out odd planks lying on the ground, flattened drums, torn sheets of tarred paper. Nothing moved. There was the noise of a lorry passing on the highway. Then silence.

If he could get to the road without being seen he would be hidden behind the evergreens. He stepped outside, stopped, and listened. Nothing. Keeping one hand on the wall, and feeling the ground with each foot before he put it down, he began to work his way slowly along the outside of the building.

Then – a noise. A foot banging against a metal drum. He froze. He couldn't tell which direction it had come from. He waited. His blood was beating so hard in his veins that he shook with it. He took another step. Somewhere, muffled by the mass of the building, there was the noise of a small piece of wood falling to the ground.

He ran.

Must get to the road! Oh God, oh God, oh God!

Something tearing out from around corner of building in opposite direction. Can't avoid!

'Ugh!'

'Ai!'

Warding-off arms tangle, overcoat shoulder crashes into chest, knee cracks into knee. A cloth cap falling. Steel-rimmed spectacles flashing as they swing out from one earpiece. Dark, anxious, short-sighted eyes closing to guard against impact. Hand groping to recover glasses.

Konstantin.

31

Under one of the street-lamps on the highway Konstantin banged the dust off his cap and bent the frame of his spectacles straight. Manning rubbed his chest where Konstantin's shoulder had hit it. They avoided meeting each other's eye.

'Well,' said Konstantin, with a short, embarrassed laugh, 'a negative conclusion. A turn of events not fully in accord with the dignity of Soviet man.'

Manning smiled foolishly, unable to think of anything to say. He felt ludicrously pleased to see someone he knew.

'An unusual way for a visitor to our country to behave,' said Konstantin. 'Running about state construction sites in the dark.'

'I lost my head.'

'One moment you were walking down the street, like a normal bourgeois intellectual. Next moment – ptut! – gone. Then five minutes later you come shooting out from nowhere like a policeman after a bribe. An untypical phenomenon.'

He threw the words away casually, almost surreptitiously, as if they were old sweet wrappers he was disposing of in the street. He settled his cap carefully back on to his head, jiggling it back and forth to get the exact fit. It occurred to Manning why Konstantin was so different in appearance from most of the other men he knew in Moscow. The others had reached 1935 in their style of dressing. Konstantin had not yet got beyond 1918.

They began to walk along the highway together. It seemed to Manning infinitely less threatening now.

'Why were you following me?' he asked.

Konstantin shrugged.

'Wanted to keep abreast of any new developments in Western book distributing technique,' he said. 'I congratulate you on getting your books back, by the way. Intelligent. Who thought of it – you or Proctor-Gould?'

'Proctor-Gould.'

'My mistake, of course, giving you the address. Mind must have steamed up a little after an hour in the dietary dining-room. Didn't strike me till we were on our way out of the National with the second case of books. Never mind – we've still got that. I need hardly say, they're not at Kurumalinskaya Street, so don't come round and break the place up again.'

'Case number one, equally, is no longer at the National.'

'Exactly. The stage of pure banditry is now at an end.'

They strode along companionably. Manning began to feel cheerful; he and Konstantin rather took to each other, he thought.

'Konstantin,' he said, 'what's all this business about?'

Konstantin looked at him sharply.

'Proctor-Gould hasn't told you?'

'He doesn't know either.'

'I think he does.'

'He says not.'

'You must have deduced, anyway.'

'I've made one or two guesses.'

Konstantin wrinkled up his nose to lift his glasses back on to the bridge of his nose.

'Guessed myself in the first place,' he said. 'I can remember the exact moment. It was at an evening reception in the History Faculty. You probably recall it. Pale sunshine slanting through the learned windows, lighting up the chalk dust in the air. Professors inclining their heads to listen to their colleagues' remarks. First this way, then that, like metronomes. The Rector himself with his hands behind his back, nodding and smiling and raising his eyebrows, and raising his eyebrows and smiling and nodding. Nothing unusual. Everything in the highest degree normal.

'Then up jumps a tiny professor with a drooping eyelid.

"Comrade historians," he says, "extend so to speak the courtesy of your attention to the Englishman Proctor-Gould who is going to tell us of his belief in peaceful co-existence."

'Applause. And up stands the Englishman Proctor-Gould, smiling benevolently and attempting to unscrew his right ear. And yourself, the Englishman Manning, inspecting the quality of workmanship in your boots.

'All right, then. Speech is spoken. And elegantly translated. I listen. "Peaceful co-existence." "Common cultural heritage." "On the one hand Shakespeare, on the other, Chekhov." "Lermontov and Balmont – descended from Scotsmen." And so on.

'Stormy applause. Stormily applaud myself. Everything the Englishman Proctor-Gould says is true. Free from negative characteristics. Couldn't be better.

'And filled with a practical desire to forge the bonds of friendship then and there, the English comrade suddenly rounds on the little professor with the drooping eyelid and presents him with a handsomely bound volume of dialectically incorrect bourgeois history. "Take," he says, "this simple volume of imperialist lies as a token of the English people's eternal esteem."

'The dwarf professor accepts it with deep gratitude and a long pair of tongs. Applause. Photographers' flashes. And before the bond of friendship has had time to cool, the professor is brandishing a silver-gilt model of Moscow University. "Be so good," he says, "as to condescend to accept this worthless, thirty-centimetres high, silver-gilt facsimile of our humble skyscraper." Thunderstorm of clapping and electronic flashes.

'And at that moment it struck me.

' "Holy God!" I thought. "This tiny brigand is handing over the precious secrets of our Soviet state for foreign gold! I can tell by the look on their faces!" '

32

It was beginning to rain. Fat, wet drops smacked down on to the pavement and roadway. Konstantin looked up to investigate, and one struck the right-hand lens of his spectacles, obliterating it entirely and making him jump.

'There's a Metro station at the end of this road,' he said. 'We might get a carriage to ourselves at this time of night. Sit back – put our feet up. Good as a suite at the Sovietskaya.'

They trotted to the station, dark splodges of wetness speckling their clothes like a rash.

'Ah,' said Konstantin, as they got into a carriage with only two old women at the other end of it. 'This is underground travel as it ought to be. Take a seat. Make yourself at home. Waiter! A bottle of champagne!'

He whipped off his glasses and polished them on the lining of his cap, his nose twitching at the absence of the accustomed weight.

'It's a good way to transmit information,' he said. 'Much better than furtively depositing it in dead letter-boxes, or hiding it in false-bottomed cigarette-lighters, or slipping it into the pocket of someone's overcoat at a party. Do something secretive and someone may spy on you. Do it in public, in front of cameras, accompanied by toasts and speeches, and no one can spy on you, because everybody's watching anyway. Open deception, openly arrived at – the secret of conjurors, businessmen, and tyrants alike.'

'And you deduced all this from the expression on their faces?'

Konstantin shrugged.

'A pure blind guess, really,' he said. 'A working hypothesis, as we natural scientists call it.'

'But you thought it was worth testing?'

'Modesty. If the system had occurred to me I was sure it

must have occurred to Western intelligence agencies, too.'

'So you got Raya to steal the presents?'

'Correct. Stole the Soviet ones first – naturally assumed the information was going out. First the silver-gilt university. Then a Spassky Tower in alabaster, a plastic sputnik, a china eagle with outspread wings, a painted wooden cigarette box, and a number of other articles repugnant to Western taste. Not a spark of reaction from Proctor-Gould. Glad to see them go, from all I could tell.'

'He was being broad-minded about Raya.'

'Then I thought, perhaps he's bringing something *in* – instructions to agents, I don't know. So we stole the Nescafé. No reaction. Stole the books – and there we were.'

They were riding on the Circle line. One by one the almost deserted stations drew level with the train, ground to a halt, and vanished again. Kievskaya, Krasnopresnenskaya, Bielorusskaya, Novoslobodskaya. Manning watched them dreamily, wondering in what tone of voice the names announced themselves, whether boastfully, apologetically, or benevolently.

'I'm sorry, Konstantin,' he said awkwardly at last. 'I don't entirely believe you.'

'In what sense, don't believe?' said Konstantin slowly, blinking at Manning.

'For a start, I don't believe your story about guessing. That was pure invention, wasn't it? And your deduction about Western intelligence. That seems reasonable as far as it goes. But there's another deduction which one can't help making at the same time – that Soviet counter-intelligence would have thought of the system, too.'

'So what conclusion do you arrive at, Paul?'

'I'm not sure, Konstantin.'

'Call me Kostik, Paul. It's more normal.'

'The conclusion that suggests itself, Kostik, is that you're working for Soviet security in some way. Perhaps in a freelance capacity. I suppose you're trying to bluff Proctor-

Gould into letting himself be blackmailed, so that somebody can use the fact of his having allowed himself to be blackmailed in order to blackmail him further.'

Konstantin didn't answer. He sat in silence from one station to the next, looking out of the window and biting his thumb-nail. Then he sighed.

'There's a lot of truth in what you say,' he said, and began to bite his thumb-nail again.

'Listen,' he said at last. 'What does a kopeck look like? It depends which side you look at it from. Raya and I, now – from your point of view we look like thieves and hooligans. But from the usual side, the Soviet side, we're respectable citizens. Raya teaches Diamat at a leading institute of higher education. I'm an aeronautical metallurgist. Raya's father is very grand – a candidate member of the Presidium. We're both Komsomol leaders. Activists. Responsible young people. We're trusted to maintain moral standards. If you want to know what sort of people we are, take the case of your friend Lippe.'

'Katerina?'

'Katerina Fyodorovna Lippe. Lippe K.F. A head stuffed with nonsense, as we activists would say. She was expelled from Komsomol for telling lies about our country to a young visitor from Austria. Expulsion from Komsomol, of course, automatically meant expulsion from the university. Who took the decision to expel her from Komsomol? Metelius R.P., then joint-secretary of the Moscow State University branch, and chairman of the committee that considered Lippe's case. And who confirmed the decision of Metelius R.P.? Churavayev K.S., member of the Executive Committee, Moscow District.'

Manning stared at Konstantin, who shrugged, and pushed his glasses up his nose.

'That's Soviet life, Paul. These things occur. As it happens, Lippe was a poor student. It could have been someone more valuable.'

'Poor old Katya.'

'Certainly.'

'Do you often break people's careers?'

'I've confirmed five expulsions. None of them entirely without reason. One man later killed himself. He'd been expelled for stealing from girls he lived with. I tell you all this not because I'm proud of it, or even because I'm ashamed of it. I just want you to have a clear picture of me from the other side.'

He sounded rather depressed.

'Anyway,' he said, 'someone guessed about Proctor-Gould. The K.G.B. – the G.R.U. I don't know. Must have put them in a difficult position. Proctor-Gould has a very high standing in this country. Close personal links with a lot of senior people in the Ministry of Foreign Affairs. People say he's a friend of Mikoyan's. Is that true?'

'I've heard it said.'

'Very difficult to make investigations without letting him know he was under suspicion. All right, search his room. But if what they were looking for was really well hidden it would mean coming back day after day. And if Proctor-Gould *was* a spy, he'd presumably have taken some precautions. People used to leave hairs in their papers, and that kind of thing. Do they still do that?'

'I've no idea.'

'I expect there's some new trick. Anyway, he'd almost certainly have found out. Disposed of the evidence. Then complained to his friends in the Foreign Ministry.'

'So they asked you?'

'They asked Raya. It's normal. A pretty girl – a loyal member of Komsomol. Working in the university like yourself. Natural for her to get to know first you, and then Proctor-Gould.'

'It was done as cold-bloodedly as that?'

'I'm afraid so, Paul. Don't be downcast. She thought you were both terribly attractive. Told me so. Thought you were both wonderful. Particularly Proctor-Gould when he flew into a rage and threw the books about. She was really very impressed.'

'The k.g.b.,' said Manning, 'just told her to go and live with Proctor-Gould?'

'They weren't quite that optimistic, Paul. They just asked her to get to know him, and see if she could get inside his room. Well, they didn't know Raya as you and I know her. They underestimated her. Each morning she used to go and report progress to a fatherly man with sciatica in a little office behind the *Izvestia* building. When she went in and told him she was actually living in Proctor-Gould's room, he jumped up like a kangaroo, he was so surprised. Brought on a violent spasm of sciatica. Almost killed him. Couldn't do anything but bend over the desk and groan for ten minutes. Then he started shaking his head and saying he had a daughter himself. Never intended Raya to stoop to immorality, he said. Nevertheless, she stayed.'

'I suppose Gordon and I both made complete fools of ourselves.'

Konstantin shrugged.

'I warned him,' said Manning. 'I thought from the first that Raya was a bit too good to be true.'

'I don't want to moralize,' said Konstantin. 'But deceivers must expect to be deceived. Spies can't complain if they're spied on.'

'This is where your thesis goes astray, Kostik. Gordon's not a spy.'

'How do you know, Paul?'

'It's not in his character.'

Konstantin waggled his head from side to side.

'Character, character,' he said. 'If you were wrong about Raya, why do you think you understand Proctor-Gould?'

'We come from similar backgrounds, Kostik. We were at the same university. And you get a certain insight into someone's mind when you interpret for him. Honestly, Kostik, I understand Gordon and you don't.'

Konstantin didn't comment. He blinked, and wrinkled his nose up.

'What you and I think doesn't really matter,' he said. 'Our security forces think Gordon is carrying espionage materials. Gordon thinks he's carrying espionage materials. Those two expert opinions are enough for our purposes.'

Manning stared at Konstantin.

'God knows what your purposes are,' he said. 'If you think Gordon's a spy, why don't you go ahead and have him arrested? Why are you arguing it out with me?'

'I shall explain.'

Suddenly Manning believed he saw the reason. A warmth ran through him, as if he had taken a draught of scalding coffee.

'You're *warning* us,' he said. 'You're giving us a chance to get out.'

33

The suggestion embarrassed Konstantin. He tore off his spectacles and began to wipe them on the lining of his cap all over again. He coughed, and muttered so rapidly that Manning found it still more difficult to catch what he was saying.

'Excuse me,' he said, 'that's not formally true. . . . Sorry to say. . . . A certain basic misunderstanding. . . .'

'What?' said Manning.

Konstantin cleared his throat and pulled the wires of his glasses back round his ears.

'Look,' he said. 'Let me explain what Raya was doing for the old man with the sciatica.'

'She was stealing Gordon's belongings.'

'By no means.'

'What?'

'Well, of course not. Do you really suppose the security services of the second most powerful nation on earth would have to resort to methods of such crudity?'

'But we both know what happened. . . .'

'You're letting yourself be dazzled by the obvious. Raya was *exchanging* Gordon's belongings. She reported to the old man what presents Gordon had in his room. He supplied her with replicas which she put in their place. Then she took the originals to the office.'

'But, Kostik . . .'

'First it was the model university, the Spassky Tower, and the rest. Then the various Russian books Proctor-Gould had been given. Then they had six tins of Nescafé flown over from England. Imagine that! Picture our agent in London. Taken off stealing the plans of submarines, and told to go out and buy six tins of Nescafé! Next they began to have copies of the English books flown in.'

'But, Kostik, I don't understand this at all. Raya *was* stealing those things. We found the books and the Nescafé in your apartment.'

Konstantin sighed.

'Private enterprise,' he said. 'Characterized by all the signs of haste and compromise that go with lack of adequate resources and proper central planning. Like many Soviet citizens, Paul, we were attempting a little private speculation over and above our commitments on behalf of the state. Result: poor quality of production. Only thing to be said in its favour – it worked, and the state enterprise didn't.'

'You were stealing the stuff unofficially?'

'Exactly. And of course we followed the usual habit of speculators – we gave priority to our private efforts. That's to say, we stole the goods first. If there was no reaction from Gordon we knew they were harmless. In which case we'd pass them on to the public sector. So we come to the books, which we estimate are not harmless. Now we have two possibilities. Either we can turn them over to the state like all the rest of the stuff. Or else we can forward not Gordon's books at all, but the books Raya was given to replace them with. That would be more likely to promote Proctor-Gould's continued prosperity. Which we do, of course, depends on Proctor-Gould.'

'How much are you asking, Kostik?'

'A lot, Paul. An opportunity like this doesn't arise every day.'

'How much is that in roubles?'

Konstantin wrinkled up his nose.

'What makes you think the price is in roubles?' he asked. 'Money isn't the only thing that people want. Some people value contentment above wealth. Some power. Some fame. Some obscurity. Also it depends what's in short supply. There are commodities in shorter supply than money in this country.'

Manning studied Konstantin's face in silence.

'I told you earlier,' Konstantin went on, 'that Raya came from a very grand family. My family was honourable as well – once. A celebrated Bolshevik family, Paul, and very proud. My maternal grandfather was one of the members of the Moscow Soviet who voted for Nogin in 1917. My paternal grandfather lost an arm fighting against Kolchak in Siberia in 1919. Then in the thirties the family was trampled into the ground. Nothing unusual. A normal phenomenon at that time. My maternal grandfather was arrested. He died in prison before he could be brought to trial. My paternal grandfather was sent to a camp. He died there. My father I can't even remember. He was called up in 1941, when I was three, and killed in the battle for Kharkov two years later.

'I was brought up by my mother and my maternal grand-mother. My grandmother was a proud woman, Paul. They

150

would have murdered her in 1936 as well as her husband, but they were ashamed to touch anyone so erect and forbidding. So my mother always believed, anyway. Grandfather's death didn't change her views at all, in any direction.

'"If you believe in the Revolution," she used to say, "remain loyal to it, however its name is disgraced." And the other thing she used to say was: "Know the truth, even if it goes with you in silence to the grave." She used to sit bolt upright on a hard chair, and when she said these things she would tremble slightly, like tempered steel under load. People like that – not our generation, Paul. She didn't speculate, as we must, whether the killing, and the lies, and the darkness were all inevitable once the violence had begun, and society had been unmade.

'So I was always brought up to distinguish the truth, and to value it, without regard to its expediency. As a result I have a craving for it. I'm like a gourmet in a chronically starving land. I hunger not just for the mass of random facts with which some starving people stuff themselves until their brains are swollen. I want information that's relevant to our condition. I want disinterested interpretations, honest commentaries.

'Don't think I reject my country, Paul. Or even reject what it has become. We can overcome our famine. I'm not cynical about Gordon's activities. If I thought they would harm Russia in any way whatsoever I should do everything in my power to destroy him. But thorough mutual espionage is a blessing to both sides. How can we politick safely against each other unless we can be sure that our true strength and intentions are known?

'Not that espionage works out quite so well in practice. The information that spies steal is always vitiated by the possibility that its sources are corrupt. Where the source of information is not open to inspection, the possibility always exists that the selection of material is deliberately misleading. Information on its own is not enough; one always needs to know its origin. Stolen secrets either confirm what their recipients already know, or they're not believed.

'And that's the position that we are in, too. The supply of information is controlled in this country. The selection we get is distorted. So the value even of the information that does get through the filter is diminished. We know nothing worth knowing about what goes on outside our frontiers. Worse – we know very little more about what goes on within them. Beyond the light of one's own personal experience – darkness. What are people thinking? What are they feeling? How do they behave? Messages of reassurance or exhortation come through. One reads between the lines. Friends pool their knowledge. But in general we live like animals, in ignorance of the world around us.

'So in despair those of us who can do so turn to the West to learn about ourselves. We use our academic status to read Western publications in the closed sections of the libraries. Visitors smuggle us books. Such information as I get hold of is seen not just by Raya and me. It's passed to a whole circle of trusted friends we have built up over the years. Our aims aren't subversive, Paul. Don't think that. Not one of us who isn't a pure Leninist. There must be dozens of similar circles in Moscow alone.

'What we're always looking for is a regular channel for information from the West. Raya and I have approached a number of regular foreign visitors – journalists, businessmen, diplomats. None of them would help. They were all frightened of damaging their standing with the Soviet authorities.

'All right, then. A man who can't get food honestly must get it by other means. Necessity can't afford scruples. So we resort to exploiting Proctor-Gould.

'I want him to expand his activities, Paul, and act as a courier for us as well. On every trip he makes to Russia I shall want him to bring certain designated books and documents. I shall also expect him to use his own initiative in finding additional material. Since he has the confidence of the Soviet authorities he can help us with very little risk to himself. And I shall hold that suitcase of books as a warranty for satisfactory service.'

Manning gazed out of the window at the hurrying dark wall of the tunnel. It evaporated suddenly into the echoing white tiles of a station. Krasnopresnenskaya. They were on their second go round.

34

It had rained all night. A weak sunlight filtered through the shifting white and grey screens of cloud, making the little concrete copies of classical statues in the Park of Culture and Rest gleam sadly among the wet bushes. The bench on which Proctor-Gould and Manning sat was damp, and each time the breeze blew, droplets of water fell from the branch above their heads. From the loudspeakers among the trees came the slow movement of a violin concerto, austere and heartbreaking. On such a morning people walked gravely with a sense that the world was well-ordered and poignant.

'That music, Paul!' sighed Proctor-Gould. 'The whole soul of Russia is in it.'

'It's Bach,' said Manning shortly. He felt very tired, as though suspended a foot above the surface of the earth, and drifting past things without ever quite making contact.

Proctor-Gould gave a little giggle. He seemed remarkably cheerful altogether, as if restored to himself. His crumpled plastic mac hung open, and Manning could see that there was fluff on his blazer again, and an egg-stain on his trousers. The range of ballpoint pens and propelling pencils had reappeared in his breast pocket. As they walked about the park earlier he had been interested, even amused by

Manning's account of his conversation with Konstantin. When Manning had explained about the substitutions, and Raya's visits to the office behind the *Izvestia* building, Proctor-Gould had laughed ruefully.

'Well, well,' he had said. 'Wheels within wheels.'

And when Manning had told him about Konstantin's demands, he had merely clicked his tongue and shaken his head.

Now Manning brought up the subject again.

'What are you going to do about it, Gordon? Konstantin said he wanted a definite assurance by this evening.'

'I'm going to get back to signing up clients, Paul. That's what I'm here for. The whole Raya incident is closed and forgotten.'

'But what about the books that Konstantin's got?'

'I haven't decided yet, Paul. I might go to the militia and charge him with stealing. I might not.'

Manning stared at him in astonishment.

'This is a great change of line, Gordon.'

'I don't have to think about protecting Raya any more.'

'But last time we talked about this, Gordon, you agreed that the books might contain something incriminating that you didn't know about.'

'I suppose they might. That rubbish-bin over there might contain the Russian Crown Jewels, wrapped up in a copy of *Pravda*. But it's not very likely.'

'And what happened to your concern about other people's property? You were prepared to pay nearly 300 roubles to get the first case of books back, just because some of them didn't belong to you.'

'All right, Paul. I'll give Konstantin the same for the second case, if he's interested in selling.'

'You don't seem very concerned about it.'

'Oh, I'm deeply concerned.'

Proctor-Gould reflected for a moment, and then began to giggle again.

'On second thoughts, Paul,' he said, 'I don't think I will buy the books back. I don't think I'll complain to the militia, either. We'll just sit tight and let him hand the books over to the security people. Think of them, Paul, sitting there examining every full stop, comma, colon, and semi-colon throughout twenty-seven books to see if it has a micro-dot stuck to it! Not to mention the dots over the i's.'

He couldn't stop tittering. The sound began to irritate Manning.

'You are a most extraordinary man, Gordon,' he said. 'One moment you're being as pompous as a bishop, and the next you're sniggering like a schoolgirl. What's come over you?'

Proctor-Gould stopped tittering, and looked into the distance.

'I suppose it's nervous relief,' he said slowly. 'For a moment this week I really did think we were sunk with all hands.'

Manning ground his shoe back and forth in the gravel.

'You mean, the first lot of books . . .' he began.

'Just one of them, Paul.'

'What was in it.'

'I don't know.'

'How do you mean, you don't know?'

'I was simply given it and told who to deliver it to. I didn't inquire about the contents, I assure you.'

'But you knew they had something to do with intelligence?'

'I knew that the man who handed me the book had something to do with intelligence.'

Manning couldn't bring himself to look at Proctor-Gould. He felt a great sense of sourness, a distaste with the world in general.

'So you were lying to me before?' he said awkwardly.

'These things involve deception. You know that, Paul.'

'But, Gordon, you gave me your word, voluntarily, that

155

you had no knowledge of anything that might incriminate you.'

'I wanted to set your mind at rest, Paul. I didn't want you to be involved in any risks that I might have been running.'

'Well, I was involved, wasn't I? And I am still. If you're caught I shall certainly be arrested too.'

'There's been some risk, certainly. . . .'

'I think you've behaved badly, Gordon, very badly.'

'I haven't asked you to accept any risk that I didn't share.'

'Gordon, you didn't *ask* me to accept the risk. You were the one who was asked. You put me in danger without my even knowing about it.'

Proctor-Gould pulled at his ear.

'I wasn't empowered to tell you about what I was doing. How could I have been? You know what happens in these cases as well as I do. Where I've done wrong is in telling you even now. I regret that. I regret it deeply. However, what's done is done. I'm sorry I had to involve you, but it's all over now. We'll go to the Kiev Station this evening and get the books out. By ten o'clock the one book that matters will be out of our hands.'

'You're giving it to someone at Sasha's dinner for the Faculty this evening?'

'Let me just say that by the time the dinner is over there will be no more risk of any sort for either of us. Is that all right, Paul?'

Manning felt a profound sense of resentment.

'It's not just the risk,' he said. 'I shouldn't have agreed to take part in a deception of this sort even if I had been asked. How can there be anything honest in the world if we behave like this?'

'Come, come, Paul. Even your friend Konstantin can see the value of espionage.'

'He may be right. But I don't want to be involved in it myself. The end may be acceptable, but the means are deceitful and mercenary.'

Proctor-Gould looked round, surprise and hurt lengthening his long face.

'Mercenary?' he said. 'Paul, you don't think I'm being paid for doing this, do you? You don't think I'm putting not only my safety but my whole career in jeopardy for a few pounds on the side?'

Manning stared at a concrete Apollo Belvedere on the other side of the path. Water dripped like representational blood from the upraised stump of its concrete arm.

'I suppose not,' he said. 'I suppose you're doing it out of some self-important idea of the public good, as a contribution to improved Anglo-Soviet relations.'

Proctor-Gould frowned.

'Don't you know how these things work, Paul?' he said. 'Don't you know how these things are arranged? Let me enlighten you. A man rings you at the office in London one day. He says he works in a department of the Foreign Office concerned with developing unofficial contacts with Russia. Would you be kind enough to meet him for lunch and give him the benefit of your experience in the matter? You have lunch with him. He asks intelligent, sympathetic questions about your job. He expresses surprise at your answers. He makes notes. Then he says, there seems to be a tremendous amount of valuable material here which could help other people who have professional contacts with Russia. Could you perhaps write it down for him in the form of a memorandum? You write the memorandum and send it to him. He rings up to say he is delighted with it. Could you possibly come to dinner some, time the following week at his flat? He has a friend in the department who has read the memorandum and would very much like to meet you and discuss one or two points arising from it. You go to dinner. The friend knows all about you already. He asks after mutual friends from Cambridge. After dinner you sit and drink whisky and soda. The friend starts to talk about your memorandum. It's so revealing and so perceptive, he says, that it makes him want to know more. What kind of people are these officials you have dealings with in Moscow? What sort of life do they lead? What are their tastes? What do they believe in? What do they want? Could you write a supplementary memorandum going into this sort of biographical detail? Perhaps at this point you begin to demur. They hasten to reassure you. They don't want the information for any ulterior motive. It's just that if Britain is to establish a real understanding with Russia, which is the best guarantee of a lasting peace, the Government must have accurate, up-to-date information about the people they are dealing with. That's all. You write the supplementary memorandum, perhaps in rather cautious terms. They are still delighted. Once again you are invited to dinner at the flat. They tell you your memorandum has gone up to ministerial level, and remark how pleasant it is to know someone who is in Moscow so often. For one thing the postal service is not very reliable. One of them has a friend there he'd like to send a little present to, if he could find someone to take it. Perhaps next time you're over you'd be kind enough to oblige? You refuse, politely. You point out that you can't afford to get involved in anything that might make the Soviet authorities suspicious, since your job depends on having their confidence. At this they become rather grave, and look at each other meaningfully. Your attitude creates rather an awkward situation, they say. Unless they continue to take the most scrupulous care to preserve security, the Soviet officials who look into these things will almost çertainly discover that you have had three meetings with British intelligence, and submitted two reports to them. British intelligence? Well, they belong to a department of it, certainly – a perfectly innocuous department, of course, dealing with more or less open information about Russia, of the sort provided by returned travellers. All the same, the Russians would probably not make much distinction between one department and another. Your hosts point out that they could scarcely recommend the continued expense of time and manpower on keeping the connexion with you secret if you are no longer working for the department. And the trouble is, they explain, that if the Russians discover you have been approached by British intelligence they will never be able to be sure that you refused to work for them. So you would certainly never get another Soviet visa. Which, they would imagine, might be rather awkward in your line of business.'

There was a silence. The music from the loud-speakers had stopped. Was it the end of the slow movement? Or had the last movement gone by as well, unnoticed?

'So you take the present?' said Manning.

'You may well decide to.'

'And perhaps bring one back?'

'Possibly.'

'How many presents have you taken back and forth?'

'That doesn't concern you, Paul.'

The music started again. It was the Komsomol march, 'Brave Boys.' The poignant late spring light changed. The day became brisk.

'I see your difficulty, Gordon,' said Manning.

'I'm glad you do, Paul.'

'But there's no reason why I should cooperate in your undertaking.'

'You're not expected to cooperate, Paul.'

'Yes, I am, Gordon. I'm expected to return you your books from the Kiev Station. As you remember, I have the ticket.'

Proctor-Gould stared at Manning, his eyes infinitely lugubrious.

'Well?' he said.

'Well,' said Manning, 'if you really are in the business you might as well bring a few presents in for Konstantin. I think they might stand a better chance of doing some good.'

Proctor-Gould went on staring at Manning in silence.

Manning looked up, caught his eye, and looked away again awkwardly.

'You're not thinking of hugging that cloakroom ticket to yourself, are you?' said Proctor-Gould.

'No,' said Manning, 'I'm thinking of giving it to Konstantin.'

35

Manning had got about four or five hundred yards from the gates of the Park of Culture and Rest when Proctor-Gould's black Chaika caught up with him. Proctor-Gould held the door open.

'Jump in, Paul,' he said.

'I'll walk, thanks, Gordon.'

He began to walk again. The driver let in his clutch and cruised along level with him, the door still open like an outspread wing, sweeping people out of the way.

'There's something I want to explain to you, Paul,' said Proctor-Gould.

'You've explained already.'

'This is something else altogether.'

Manning stopped.

'Well, for God's sake get out of that car,' he said. 'The whole street's staring at us.'

Proctor-Gould scrambled out, and planted himself squarely in front of Manning, his hands in his blazer pockets, his great eyes fixed anxiously on Manning's face.

'What is it, then?' said Manning.

'Paul, I'm afraid I wasn't really telling you the truth back there in the park.'

'Oh, Gordon . . .'

'I had a very good reason for keeping the real situation to myself, as you'll see. . . .'

He stopped, and looked round. A small crowd was beginning to collect about them, staring intently into their faces, perhaps thinking, from the manner in which Manning was edging away, and Proctor-Gould crowding in upon him, that they were about to fight. The more private Proctor-Gould's disclosures became, thought Manning, the more public were the surroundings in which he chose to make them. He would end up telling the ultimate secrets of his heart from the top of the university skyscraper through a public address system. Manning looked round.

'There's a beer house just down the road,' he said. 'Let's go there.'

It was crowded inside the beer house. There were no chairs or stools, and the customers stood at shelves along the wall eating bread and cheese and drinking out of paper cups. In one corner two men were embracing each other with laughter and tears. 'We haven't seen each other for twenty years,' they kept explaining to the other customers, who smiled, and wagged their heads, and winked.

'Abstemious lot here,' said Proctor-Gould as they queued at the counter. 'They're all buying fruit juice.'

'You haven't been inside one of these places before?' said Manning, surprised.

Proctor-Gould shook his head. He looked vaguely round the room. Under the signs saying: 'It is forbidden to bring and consume spirits,' the customers were busy emptying their paper cups of fruit juice into the ash-trays, and refilling them from half-bottles of vodka they carried in their pockets. But Proctor-Gould was already thinking about something else.

'Paul,' he said, in a low voice which made several men in the queue turn round and gaze at them expressionlessly. 'You didn't really believe all that stuff I told you about getting involved with British intelligence, did you?'

Manning looked at him carefully.

'Yes, I did,' he said.

Proctor-Gould smiled.

'Rather cloak-and-dagger for your taste, I should have thought,' he said.

'It sounded about right to me.'

'I obviously have a career as a story-teller. Because it wasn't the truth, Paul. The truth is rather simpler. If I may give you a tip, it usually is.'

They collected two paper cups of beer, and found themselves a space at the shelf.

'Go on, then,' said Manning. 'Let's have the new version.'

'It's soon told, Paul,' said Proctor-Gould, leaning along the counter towards Manning and talking in the same low voice. 'As you know, there are a number of what are called "underground" writers in this country. They work in secret, and their manuscripts are smuggled out of the country and published in the West.'

Manning looked up from his beer, met Proctor-Gould's unblinking gaze, and looked away again, disconcerted.

'Now,' said Proctor-Gould, 'somebody else – I don't know who – arranges for the manuscripts to be got out. I'm part of a chain which brings the royalties back to the author. That may sound mercenary to you, Paul, like everything else, but these people are no different from any other writers – they have to live. I don't know the author in question myself – I don't even know his pen-name in the West. All I know is that I'm given a book with a number of 100 dollar bills made up inside the binding, and that I'm due to hand it over to the next link in the chain tonight. I believe there are some cuttings of reviews with the money, too. I don't know whether you think this sort of operation is worthwhile, Paul?'

'Oh, yes.'

'It seems so to me, I must say. I'm glad you agree. I'd be very grateful, Paul, if you'd go to the Kiev Station some time before the dinner this evening and get that case out of the left luggage office for me.'

Manning sipped a little of his beer. It tasted like dilute Syrup of Figs.

'I'm afraid I don't believe you, Gordon,' he said.

'I think you do, Paul.'

'Why did you tell me the other version?'

Proctor-Gould sighed.

'Once I'd admitted that one of the books contained something – which I should never have done – I had to go on and complete the story. At the time it didn't seem to matter what you thought of me as a result, provided only that (*a*) you believed the story, and that (*b*) it wasn't the truth. I obviously made rather too good a job of it; you not only believed the story – you struck moral attitudes about it. Now that you've forced me to tell you the true version I want your solemn oath that you will not divulge it to any-one – not hint at it – not even refer to it obliquely when you are back in England. Will you give it me, please?'

He was leaning close to Manning. It reduced his height, so that he was looking up into Manning's face, his earnest brown irises underlined by the whites and the pink rim beneath them. On either side of the two Englishmen the line of jawbones champed up and down, the guzzling Adam's apples wobbled stolidly on.

'It's ridiculous to give my word,' said Manning, 'if I don't believe the story.'

'I want your word whether you believe it or not.'

'All right, then,' said Manning reluctantly. It seemed to him that in giving his word he was also implying his accept-ance of the story. He would have liked to make it clear to Proctor-Gould that he reserved his opinion, but it seemed a hopelessly complicated point to explain to those straight-forward brown eyes.

'You swear?' said Proctor-Gould.

'Yes, yes.'

' "I swear"?'

'I swear.'

163

Proctor-Gould straightened up.

'Even if you're not convinced,' he said, 'I hope I've managed to sow doubts. In any case, Paul, I don't think you'd really give your pal Konstantin the means of blackmailing me, would you? After all, come wind, come rain, we *are* fellow-countrymen. In fact we're fellow-Johnsmen.'

He smiled at Manning ruefully.

'I'm not coming the old blood-is-thicker-than-water, I assure you,' he said. 'All the same, one does have a certain undeniable leaning towards one's compatriots, doesn't one? One doesn't deliberately set out to sell them into the hands of foreigners.'

Manning swallowed the rest of his beer. It made him shudder. Proctor-Gould, he noticed, had not even touched his.

'I'll think about it,' he said.

36

The faculty looked curiously unimpressive around the dinner table, thought Manning. Ginsberg, Romm, Rubeshchenskaya, Skorbyatova, even Korolenko himself – they all seemed tamed and domesticated among the starched napery, the ranks of crystal glasses and the podgy wives. The personalities which were so distinctive on the dusty lecture rostrum each day had faded, the repertoire of famous mannerisms laid aside. For one thing, they were all dominated by the architecture of the room. It was in one of the banqueting suites of the university skyscraper. Pillars of veined blood-red soapstone supported complex funereal urns. Fluted gilt columns flowered into clusters of flambeaux. Triple-tiered chandeliers hung down from the dark upper air. Amidst it all, mere lounge-suited flesh and blood looked pallid and unsatisfactory.

Manning felt as pallid as the others looked. He was very tired, brought low by the strains of the last few days. Mrs Skorbyatova was saying something to him. He could not be bothered to take it in. He would have liked to lower his head until his chin was resting discreetly on his chest, and then close his eyes for five or ten minutes. It occurred to him that he was starting to get noticeably drunk. Well, to hell with it.

Romm was on his feet, holding up his glass. Another toast. 'The London School of Civic Studies.' How did the London School of Civic Studies come into it, so far away around the bend of the world? Never mind. Pick up the little vodka glass. Lift. Clink against Mrs Skorbyatova's glass on his left, and Mrs Loyeva's on his right. Mumble. Tip draught down throat in one blazing, fuming stream. Hold breath. Drink mineral water before the suffocating fumes rose and choked him. Already the waitresses were recharging the glasses for the next toast.

He took a deep breath, and began to examine the faces around the table. Rubeshchenskaya was talking to Korolenko. Her plain, honest face bobbed up and down, wagged from side to side, raised its eyebrows, talked and talked. Korolenko listened in silence, motionless and expressionless. Now Rubeshchenskaya had stopped, and was looking at Korolenko interrogatively. The spasm lifted the right-hand corner of his mouth for an instant. As if it were an acknowledgement she smiled and nodded, and went on talking.

On the other side of Rubeshchenskaya sat Proctor-Gould. Then a little sharp-faced woman with grey hair, who was probably Mrs Korolenko, and next to her, Sasha. Proctor-Gould and Sasha were leaning forward to talk to each other across Mrs Korolenko. Sasha was listening anxiously, blinking a little, as if frightened of missing a word. Proctor-Gould was speaking with little smiles, and chopping motions of his right hand. Occasionally he turned his head a little more sharply, and directed one of the smiles at Mrs Korolenko.

She acknowledged each of them with a small, unamused smile of her own, making no attempt to understand the English conversation.

Manning realized that Mrs Skorbyatova was looking at him, a humorous expression on her large, oval face.

'Don't you think so?' she was asking.

Manning laughed politely.

'I suppose I do,' he said.

He couldn't take his eyes off Proctor-Gould's face. It was as familiar as an old sock, so familiar that it embarrassed him. It was like seeing one's mother at a school speech day. How could anyone take that homely face seriously? At any moment Proctor-Gould would pull his ear. As if by telepathy, he pulled it at once – a long, surreptitious, caressing tug. Oh God, it was shaming to watch!

Among the flowers on the table in front of Proctor-Gould lay four books, neatly stacked. He had come to Manning's room in Sector B just before the dinner and selected them from the suitcase which Manning had brought back from the station.

'Thank you, Paul,' he had said. Manning had shrugged. Proctor-Gould had looked as if he was going to say something else about Manning's decision to cooperate, then changed his mind and glanced perfunctorily about the room instead.

'Nice place you've got here.'

'Yes.'

'Your own bathroom?'

'Shared with the room next door.'

'Very well arranged. A bit different from poor old John's.'

'Yes.'

'It's odd, really, Paul. I've never seen your room before. You must invite me out here some time and show me over the whole building.'

A formal occasion. But now, in public Manning felt that

the burden of intimacy was not quite so easily laid down. Proctor-Gould had humiliated himself in front of him with his deceit. It made a continuing claim upon him.

Ginsberg was on his feet, proposing a toast to friendly cooperation in the field of human administration. Up glass. Clink Skorbyatova, clink Loyeva. 'Field of huministration.' Down vodka. Gulp mineral water. Ah. Belch. Excuse me. Ah.

Korolenko was standing up. Another toast? Scarcely – glasses not yet recharged. Speech, undoubtedly. Was indeed already speaking. But what was he saying? Manning found it almost impossible to focus his mind on the words.

'... sometimes falls to our lot to have the *plea*sure of welcoming into our midst one whose aims and aspi*ra*tions are entirely in accord with the *spir*it of peaceful co-exist-ence. Such a one is un*doubt*edly our distinguished and re-spected guest Proctor-*Gould*. . . .'

Korolenko stood with his hands behind his back, erect and exact, speaking in a quiet level voice without expression of any sort, apart from the regular stresses with which he marked the passage of time. This was his Essential Attributes of the Soviet Administrator voice, characterized by its com-plete dissociation from sense and matter, uncontaminated by the personal interest which he took in such questions as barring the admission of unauthorized persons to the Faculty canteen. Occasionally, on one of the stressed syllables, he would rock gently forward on to his toes, as soldiers do on long parades to keep their blood in circulation. Everyone sat straight in his chair, staring into space with glazed eyes, stunned with respect and boredom and vodka. Manning tried to imagine Korolenko drunk. It was difficult. He visualized him with his brother officers in some derelict commandeered house in occupied territory, impassively tipping back vast quantities of spirit at the end of the day. It made no difference. Perhaps he became even more erect, more expressionless. Perhaps his eyelids came down a little.

Perhaps he renounced speech altogether, until the occasional sardonic spasm was the only sign of continued life. . . .

Time hung suspended. . . .

Now Korolenko was lifting a volume bound in white leather from among the flowers on the table in front of him, and holding it up while he spoke, wagging it slightly like a swollen forefinger at each stress. Now he was turning to Proctor-Gould, who was standing up uncertainly, unable to understand the Russian. Korolenko was handing him the book. Now he was clapping, and both sides of his mouth were elevated in a smile.

They all applauded. Korolenko offered a toast to Proctor-Gould. Everyone gulped it down and turned to his neighbour to start talking hurriedly and meaninglessly in his relief that the speech was over.

'Well, well,' said Mrs Skorbyatova.

'There we are, then,' said Manning.

Someone was calling his name.

'Paul! Paul!'

Where . . . ? Ah, Proctor-Gould. The familiar old face was thrust towards him across the table.

'Paul,' it said, 'I'm going to make a speech. Would you oblige with your usual skilful services?'

'Tiny bit drunk, Gordon,' said Manning.

'Little hazy myself, to tell you the truth. Never mind – all add to the gaiety of the occasion. Come round and stand next to me.'

Manning got to his feet. The room keeled steadily over to port. Christ. He took hold of the edge of the table and waited for it to come back on to the level. Not funny. Didn't know I was quite as bad as that.

He edged his way round the table, holding on to the backs of the chairs, until he reached Proctor-Gould's. All right now. Lean myself on the back of the chair like this. Be as steady as a rock.

'All right?' asked Proctor-Gould, looking up at him.

'Ready when you are.'

Proctor-Gould cleared his throat and stood up. Immediately the chair capsized under Manning's weight and deposited him on the floor.

'Are you all right?' asked Sasha anxiously, helping him up, among the applause for Proctor-Gould.

'Fine.'

'Sure you're all right, Paul?' This was Proctor-Gould.

'Perfectly.'

Proctor-Gould turned back to the table.

'Dean Korolenko, Mrs Korolenko, ladies and gentlemen,' he said. 'It is indeed a great honour, of which I am very conscious, to be invited to share with such a distinguished body of men and women an occasion of this nature. I am not myself, of course, a member of the international fraternity of administration experts. I am a humble British businessman, and my only claim upon your time and attention is that I have been entrusted with a number of commissions from my many friends in the learned institutions engaged on similar work in Britain.'

He stopped, and half-turned towards Manning to wait for the translation. Manning blinked. What the hell had Proctor-Gould been saying? He couldn't remember the half of it.

'He's very pleased to be here,' he said uncertainly. 'At an occasion of this nature he recalls that he has many friends in learned institutions engaged on similar work in Britain.'

Proctor-Gould was frowning at him.

'What do you think you're up to, Paul?' he whispered.

'Got the general sense of it,' muttered Manning defensively.

'You were speaking English. Do you realize that?'

'Gordon, I wasn't!'

'You were.'

'Was I?'

'Yes.'

'Oh God.'

He hurriedly tried again in Russian, and the speech continued. But the more he translated, the more obsessed he became with his lapse, and the insight it had given Proctor-Gould into his standards of accuracy as an interpreter. And the more he worried about that, the less he heard or remembered of what Proctor-Gould was saying, and the more he had to improvise. It was like a nightmare in which his appalled gazing back at each last disaster brought him blundering into the next.

Now Proctor-Gould was taking up the four books from the table one by one and presenting them.

'For Professor Rubeshchenskaya,' Manning heard himself translating, 'a small memento from her friends in the department at Edinburgh. . . . For Sasha Zaborin, a volume of his beloved Schubert songs from his old pupils Michael Sloane and Trevor Westland. . . . For Dean Korolenko, a bound volume of the *Proceedings of the Institute of Civic Studies*, from the Director and staff of the Institute . . . And lastly . . .'

But for whom the last volume was destined Manning didn't quite catch. He was in the process of descending from the remoteness of the sky into a chair which had somehow appeared to catch him.

'You'll feel better sitting down,' said a gentle, anxious voice. Manning could see Sasha's thin, wind-blown hair somewhere at the edge of his field of vision.

'Come over a bit funny,' he said.

'You'll be all right.'

'Making a fool of myself.'

'Russian hospitality. It happens to everyone.'

Events became confused, as if in another world. Manning had an impression of applause, of glasses clinking, of laughter. At some stage the chairs were pushed back. People were moving about. Faces bent over him.

'Hallo,' he said to them, smiling.

One of the faces was Korolenko's.

'Your friend Lippe,' it seemed to be saying, 'is ill. She was found in the street. She was taken to the First City Hospital.'

'Thank you,' said Manning.

More faces. People leaving the room. Other people coming into the room. Manning caught a glimpse of Proctor-Gould. Old Gordon seemed to be in a bad way as well. Two men in overcoats were holding his elbows. His face was very white.

Then arms were placed under his own armpits, lifting him to his feet, helping him towards the door.

'Thank you,' he said. 'Very kind. Bit tricky at the moment.'

He swivelled his head to see who it was helping him. Not anyone he knew. Two men in overcoats. Friends of friends, perhaps.

Outside the door in one of the great marble corridors of the university, he saw Sasha. He was talking to another man in an overcoat, looking over the man's shoulder and frowning anxiously at Manning.

'Sorry, Sasha,' said Manning.

Farther on down the corridor Konstantin was hovering.

'Sorry, Kostik,' said Manning. 'Ashamed to be seen by you in this condition. I truly am.'

Konstantin shook his head and waved his hand deprecatingly.

'Never kept our appointment,' said Manning. 'Sorry, Kostik.'

Konstantin was left behind. They were going down a broad staircase. People were staring. Manning's feet muddled up the edges of the stairs, tumbling over them inertly. He felt infinitely sad and ashamed.

'Sorry,' he told the men who were holding him. 'God, I'm sorry!'

He began to cry.

Outside the night was blessedly cool and dark. Down, down the unending flight of ceremonial stairs to the roadway. He was being put into the back of a car. Then the car was full of silent men in overcoats, smelling of scent and cigarettes and sweat.

'Put his head down,' said one of them, as the car accelerated across the piazza. 'He's going to be sick.'

37

Manning's acclimatization to captivity was softened for him; on the first day the prison took its place as one more of the after-effects of drunkenness – intimate, timeless, and unreal. By the second day it already felt natural, and indeed inevitable.

There seemed to be no one else in his section of the prison. From the little exercise yard where he was taken for an hour each morning he could sometimes hear the noises of human activity – a shout, someone laughing, a bucket scurring along a stone floor. But he saw no one except the warders who unlocked him and brought him his food. The food was not very much worse than it had been in the Faculty canteen. He was still wearing his own clothes, though his belt, tie, watch and money had disappeared, and the laces had been removed from his shoes. Someone had fetched a few of his belongings and placed them in his cell; he had his own toothbrush and his own shaving tackle, though the blades had gone. Each morning he was unlocked and allowed to slop along in his unlaced shoes to the ablutions at the end of the corridor – a lavatory without a seat or a door, and a sink with a cold tap and a block of hard, cheese-coloured soap. The duty warder fitted one of his confiscated blades into the razor for him, and waited while he made his toilet. All he lacked was a towel. By some administrative oversight, none of his own towels had been included with his belongings, and none was issued by the prison, so that he was forced to dry his hands on his one spare handkerchief, which quickly became sodden.

His sense of isolation and unrelatedness was increased because he did not know where the prison was. He was fairly certain that it was not the Lubianka, where foreign prisoners were usually taken. The outside of the Lubianka was like a large office block, and people said the cells were underground. His own cell was on the first floor, and so far as he could see from the exercise yard the building was more like some sort of old-fashioned penitentiary. He was not even sure that he was still in Moscow. The car ride had seemed to last an eternity. All he could remember about it was being repeatedly, shamefully sick.

He asked the warders who came to unlock him, or to inspect him through the peep-hole, where the prison was, but they never answered. He asked them if Proctor-Gould was in the same prison. They ignored that, too. He asked them what he was charged with. He asked to see someone from the British Embassy. He asked for paper to write to his mother. He asked for a towel. The warders went on with what they were doing as if they had not heard. The questions began to sound foolish even to Manning.

He wondered if the Embassy knew about their arrest. Unless the police had notified them, he thought probably not – at any rate, not yet. There was no one who could have told them. Sasha or Konstantin might have been prepared to, but Russians would not normally be able to communicate with a Western embassy. It was possible, anyway, that Konstantin had been arrested himself at the end of the Faculty dinner. As if from a dream Manning could remember him standing in a corridor . . . shaking his head at something Manning was saying. . . .

Proctor-Gould's disappearance would soon be noticed, of

course, even if his own was not. Manning tried to remember if he had mentioned any appointments with Embassy people, or with people who might be expected to inform the Embassy if he failed to turn up. Proctor-Gould had too many links and contacts for his absence to go unremarked for more than a day or two at most. Then the Embassy would take action. It was the sort of job they would give to Chylde, who used to invite Manning to his parties. Manning tried to imagine Chylde taking action. He pictured Chylde's face, all pink and smooth, and heard Chylde's voice, humbly distributing the alms of his benevolent interest to all those less fortunate creatures in the world who through some unfortunate deficiency of taste, education, nationality, or character had not been selected for the British Foreign Service. It was not an entirely reassuring thought.

Manning struck up some sort of acquaintance with the warder on night duty. He was older than the other warders, and he had sagging shoulders, with a crumpled face set in an expression of permanent apology. When he came on duty in the evening he would slide back the peep-hole and ask:

'All right, son?'

Manning was encouraged by these few words in the silence. He took to asking to be let out to the lavatory each evening; constipated by the impersonal stares of the day warders, he found he could manage to empty his bowels in the night man's more sympathetic presence. One evening, as he sat on the lavatory, the night man took a cigarette out of his tunic pocket, cut a third of it off with his pocket-knife, lit the two pieces in his own mouth, and gave the smaller one to Manning.

'Stop the smell,' he said. 'Always light up in the lavatory myself.'

'Thanks,' said Manning. He was moved by the gesture.

'What have they got you for, son?' asked the night man.

'I don't know.'

The night man chuckled humourlessly.

' "I don't know",' he mimicked.

They smoked in silence. The night man stood with his head turned to one side, as if listening for some faint, distant sound. Manning took the opportunity to repeat his various requests. 'Mother,' 'Embassy,' 'towel,' – the words echoed away ridiculously down the corridor from the doorless lavatory, under the weak, bare bulbs in their wire guards. The night man did not even look at Manning. Whatever the sounds were that his ear was cocked to catch, they were not Manning's complaints.

But one point had got through, at any rate. When Manning had reached the stage of washing his hands, and drying them on the sodden handkerchief, the night man took the end of his cigarette out of his mouth between his second finger and thumb, and flushed it carefully away down the lavatory. Then he said:

'Should have a towel. To dry yourself.'

'Can you get me one?'

'Not my job, son.'

'Couldn't you tell someone . . . ?'

'No one to tell on this shift.'

Some of the time, as Manning sat on the bed in his cell, watching the patch of sunlight from the window creep millimetre by millimetre across the wall, lengthening, then at last reddening, fading, and disappearing, he felt despair. He was abandoned. No one knew where he was. He had fallen off the edge of the world.

But more often he worried. Not so much about whether a charge would be brought against him, or what sentence he would get if it was. These eventualities still seemed remote and improbable. He worried about what would happen when he was taken out of his cell, as he assuredly soon would be, and questioned.

Over and over again he tried to visualize the scene. He imagined that the questioner would be in uniform, but hatless, sitting at a desk in a small room. However the external circumstances changed in his imagination, the questioner's face remained the same. It was someone exactly like Sasha – anxious, courteous, scrupulous, demanding, personally wounded by any deviation from his own standards of honesty and frankness. Or so, at any rate, he would seem.

At first he would be sympathetic and amiable. He would shake hands. Offer Manning a cigarette. Ask how he was being treated. Manning imagined that he might tell him about not having a towel. The man would apologize. Would promise to get him one.

Then he would ask Manning when he had first met Proctor-Gould. What was the exact nature of the duties he had accepted? What financial arrangement had they come to? Whom had he met in the course of his work as Proctor-Gould's interpreter? On which dates? Where? The answers to all these questions would be known to the interrogator already, since it had all been done in public, in front of witnesses, within range of microphones. Manning would tell the truth so far as he could remember it. It would tally with the record. The interrogator would remain sympathetic and amiable.

Then, at some stage, he would be asked if Proctor-Gould had ever told him the nature of the secret work upon which he was engaged.

What would he say?

If he said yes he would incriminate not only Proctor-Gould but himself, as Proctor-Gould's accessory.

If he said no . . .

Manning could see the puzzled, hurt look come into the interrogator's eyes, as it did sometimes into Sasha's. Manning had never asked Proctor-Gould what he was up to? – No. He had helped Proctor-Gould force an entry into the apartment on Kurumalinskaya Street in order to recover his books by force, and he had not asked for any explanation? – Well, Proctor-Gould had said it was because the books had been entrusted to his care by his clients. Who were his clients? – Proctor-Gould hadn't specified. Manning had accepted that explanation? – Yes.

The interrogator would get up from his desk and go across to the window. With his back to him he would ask quietly: was there nothing that Manning wished to add to his answer? No. And thereafter the questioner's sympathy and amiability would be gone. Thereafter Manning would be treated, rightly, as a liar.

Manning felt his palms moisten at the thought. No doubt, if they felt he was concealing something really important, they would proceed to harsher methods of questioning. They would bully him. They would keep him awake at night, reduce his diet, make threats. They might very well go further. But already Manning doubted if he had the moral fortitude to resist such complete isolation from sympathy and approval. Wouldn't it be better to tell them the whole truth in the first place? To be cooperative, to admit he had been wrong? To say he had done it only so as not to betray a comrade? To be ashamed, to ask for clemency?

He did not think he owed any further loyalty to Proctor-Gould, or to the ridiculous oath he had been made to swear. Proctor-Gould had involved him without his consent. He had tried to compel his continued cooperation by telling him two entirely different stories, both of which could not be true. And what version was he offering his interrogators even now, wherever he was? Perhaps it was one which attempted to make Manning out to be the principal. It was impossible to know – he might be trying to exculpate Manning entirely. Manning built structures of indignation and guilt on each hypothesis in turn. But it did not help with the practical question of what he was going to tell the interrogator. He could not guess how Proctor-Gould was likely to behave. Under the shifting sands of explanation and counter-explanation, he realized, he had no idea what sort of person Proctor-Gould was at all.

'When are they going to question me?' Manning asked the night man as he sat on the lavatory smoking another third of a cigarette.

'Impatient, are you?' said the night man.

'I'd like to know.'

'We'd all like to know a lot of things. Have they issued you with a towel yet?'

'No.'

'You want to get the towel straight first, son. If you can't even get a towel to dry yourself on there's not much point in worrying your head about legal matters.'

Then again, even if he decided what to say about Proctor-Gould, it didn't end his difficulties. Supposing he was asked about Konstantin and Raya? The security people must have realized that Raya was stealing the books as well as exchanging them. And Proctor-Gould had probably told his interrogator everything that Manning had relayed to him of Konstantin's activities. Was there any possible point for Manning in trying to deny all knowledge of those activities? Wouldn't it just make his own position worse without in any way helping Konstantin or Raya? Raya's father could probably protect them more effectively than he could hope to.

From his own experience it was always better in the end to be honest. Indeed, he had almost no experience of attempting anything but honesty. All ethical aspects apart, wasn't he simply too unpractised to resort to deceit now? Anyway, if he was not whole-hearted in his attempt to deceive – and he was not – he would not have the slightest chance of being believed. And by being detected in deceit he would make things worse not only for himself, but for all four of them. . . .

He worried, and drowsed on his bed. When he awoke the problems were still there to be worried about, more concrete, more complex and interconnected hour by hour. He would have liked to talk about them with the night man, and because he could not, their evening conversations languished, and became one-sided and single-track. They talked about almost nothing but the towel; Manning's continued failure to provide himself with one provoked ever more pained and eloquent admonitions.

'You want to exert yourself, you know,' the night man would say. 'Make a formal complaint through the proper channels. If that doesn't work, make another complaint. Take it up to the central administration, if necessary. You've got rights, you know, son. We're not living under the cult of personality now. It's not healthy, wiping your hands on that little handkerchief all the time. Ah, you're all the same, you youngsters – you just won't make the effort.'

On some days Manning was resolved to say nothing that might incriminate anyone. On other days he made up his mind to tell the whole truth and save his skin as best he could. Then there were times when he settled on a more pragmatic approach. He would say nothing incriminating until it definitely became clear from the course of the interview that this was doing him more harm than good. But by then, of course, he would have destroyed his credit. He became obsessed with the fear that even if he told his questioners the truth they would not believe it, or would not accept it as being complete, and would go on pressing him for information which he did not have.

After a while he found it difficult to keep track of the days. The warders were taken off his section, replaced by fresh men, and then brought back, according to some rota that he could not follow. The night man was off for five nights, back for four, then off for three. Some days Manning was taken to the bath-house, at a time when no one else was using it, and allowed to take a supervised bath. Twice this happened on a Tuesday. After his third bath it took him an hour to work out that it was not a Tuesday at all this time but a Monday.

In the bath-house he was always issued with a towel to

dry himself, but each time it had to be handed in again, in spite of his protests. He did his best to keep the handkerchief in his cell clean, and to get it dried out, but his face and hands became chapped, and the chaps became sores.

'I told you it was a disgusting habit,' said the night man, shaking his head. 'Let this be a lesson to you, son.'

Then he got some form of stomach trouble, and had to shout for the warder two or three times an hour to take him to the lavatory. The smell of his motions drove even the night man away, in spite of his cigarette. He ran a temperature, and his anxieties boiled up inside his head. They seemed like vessels driven round in a maelstrom, spinning and swirling and colliding, appearing, and disappearing, changing their shape entirely. He asked repeatedly to see a doctor, and eventually one came. But by that time the fever had subsided. All the same, it was a pleasure to see someone who wasn't a warder. And afterwards a series of orderlies arrived in his section, bringing a tonic for him to take, an ointment for his sores, a stack of English classics in Russian translation with half their pages torn or missing – and a towel. He lay on his bed feeling very low, taking the tonic three times a day after meals, listlessly reading the books, and planning how to make the towel last. The weather was fine. The tiny patch of sky he could see through the high window was blue every day, and the cell became uncomfortably hot in the afternoons. His anxiety about what he would say when he was questioned faded from his mind, and became entirely forgotten. He settled into a quiet round of unhappiness, sweeping out his cell and exercising once a day, bathing once a week, dreaming of his mother's house and talking about it each evening to the night man. The night man listened only perfunctorily; now that Manning had got a towel he had rather lost interest in him.

It was the night man who woke him one morning at dawn, switching on the light in his cell while the high rectangle of the window was still pale grey.

'Clothes on, son, and get your belongings together,' he said, in his companionable voice. 'I want you outside in the corridor ready for transfer in two minutes.'

38

The night man took him out of his private section and through the main body of the prison, unlocking and re-locking each door they passed through. They crossed an open yard, the night man silently leading the way. Slopping along in his unlaced shoes, Manning had some difficulty in keeping up with him. In the grey half-light he could see odd groups of men in prison overalls slouching away towards the other side of the yard – perhaps on their way to the kitchens to start preparing breakfast. The air was cold. Manning shivered.

They went into a large office with a stone floor, and a bare electric bulb shining down on ugly brown tables and filing cabinets. There were a number of men in the room, some in uniform, some wearing civilian clothes; some sitting down at the tables, some standing with their hands in their overcoat pockets.

'Hallo, Paul,' said one of them in English. Manning had difficulty for a moment in distinguishing which of them had spoken. Then he saw; it was Sasha. He opened his mouth to reply, but his vocal chords seemed to be inert.

A man sitting at a table pushed a slip of paper and a pen across to Manning.

'Sign this,' he said.

Manning signed, blindly. It could have been a fictitious deposition, or his own death warrant. The man slid a rough brown paper parcel across to him and opened it briefly for him to see. Manning caught a glimpse of his tie, his watch, and a pile of loose change. The man pulled out a pair of shoe laces and tossed them to Manning.

'Lace up your shoes,' he said.

Fumblingly, Manning crammed the laces through the holes, conscious of nothing but the indifferent gaze of everyone in the room. Then one of the men in civilian clothes opened the door for him, and he was taken out into a dark, echoing archway. A picket door was unlocked with a tremendous clatter. Manning looked round to see if he could see the night man among the figures about him, to say good-bye, but in the poor light he couldn't pick him out. He stumbled as he stepped through the picket.

They were in the street. A modest Pobyeda saloon stood at the kerb, and they got into it, one man on either side of Manning on the back seat, and Sasha next to the driver.

Sasha at once turned round and gazed at Manning in the twilight. He compressed his lips, then leant over and squeezed Manning's hand.

'It's good to see you, Paul,' he said in Russian. He sounded moved, and he was blinking awkwardly. Manning nodded back, for some reason still unable to say anything. Sasha looked away.

'Was it bad in there?' Sasha asked. Manning began to shake his head, then nodded once. Suddenly he was seized by the dawn coldness, and began to shudder violently. Without a word Sasha struggled out of his overcoat and pulled it round Manning's shoulders.

'All right?' said the driver.

'All right,' said Sasha.

The car moved off, and drove slowly up the empty street. They passed women sweeping the gutters, and at the corner a dozen people waiting for a bus, their faces all turned the same way in expressionless expectation.

'We're going to Sheremetyevo,' said Sasha. 'You have a seat booked aboard the 8.30 a.m. flight to London.'

'I'm being deported?'

'Yes. You'll be at London by half past ten. We collected

182

all your stuff from your room and packed it up – it's in the boot. Your thesis and all your notes are in the small brown case. Is there anything you want me to collect from anywhere else to send on later?'

Manning shook his head. They drove slowly through the eastern suburbs into the centre of Moscow, not talking. The sky was growing light. Manning caught a glimpse of the university skyscraper floating over the city on the Sparrow Hills, already brilliantly sunlit, the illuminated red star on its pinnacle extinguished against the perfectly cloudless summer sky. At an intersection in the north of the city the sun burst into the car, shining straight down a long boulevard opening from their right, dazzling them. To Manning the streets and the sunlight looked as ordinary and expected as the walls of his cell. He had not yet adjusted to his sudden release. All he felt was a certain dull irritation that he had not been given time to shave before leaving.

'We're going to have a lot of time in hand,' said Sasha. 'I don't know whose idea it was, starting this early. Perhaps we'll be able to get breakfast at the airport.'

The car cruised slowly out to the north-west. Manning wanted to ask about Konstantin and Raya, but felt that it might imply that he knew of some reason why they should be in trouble. It might be wrong to inquire even about Katerina.

'What's happening to Proctor-Gould?' he asked eventually.

'I don't know, Paul.'

'He was arrested?'

'Oh, yes. You haven't heard any of the details?'

'I haven't been told anything.'

'Korolenko was arrested, too, of course.'

'Korolenko? Have either of them been charged?'

'I don't know. There was a lot about it in the papers for a start. It's all public knowledge – I don't suppose it matters if I tell you.'

He glanced at one of the men sitting next to Manning. The man raised his eyebrows disclaimingly, and looked out of the window.

'It was all to do with those books which Gordon was presenting at the Faculty dinner that night,' said Sasha. 'Apparently the police had examined them beforehand. According to the papers, the books had been in a suitcase which you had deposited at the Kiev Station. I don't know whether that's right. . . ?'

'Yes.'

'Well, the police took the case away from the station, examined the books, and then replaced them in the left luggage office in order to see who they were intended for. The police said that the book which Proctor-Gould gave to Korolenko had a very heavy binding in which there was some money concealed.'

Manning looked out of the window, warmed and dazzled by the serene sunlight which shot into the car between each building shadow. So it had been royalties after all. The terrible deviousness which Proctor-Gould had imposed upon himself was entirely quixotic. Manning remembered the various moral attitudes he had struck about him, and felt ashamed.

At Sheremetyevo Manning opened the brown paper parcel and put on his tie. They got fresh ham rolls at the buffet, and when the girl had raised steam in the Espresso machine, large capuccino coffees.

'It's rather ironical, coming to the airport like this to see you off,' said Sasha. 'I told Gordon at that dinner that I was ready to go to England as one of his clients.'

'Oh,' said Manning.

They sat, waiting for time to pass. Sasha told Manning the Faculty gossip, but to Manning it sounded unreal and dull, like the annals of some village club. He got permission to go to the men's room under the supervision of one of the guards to shave.

He had his face close to the mirror, and was absorbed in trying not to breathe and steam up the last few clear inches of the glass, when a finger came between himself and his reflection. He stared at it. In the condensation on the mirror it scribbled a six-pointed squiggle, like two cursive w's – 'shsh' – then deleted it, and was immediately withdrawn.

Manning slowly straightened up, and without turning his head looked into the mirror above the wash-basin next to his. The face reflected in it was Konstantin's. They gazed at each other in the mirror, neither of them giving any sign of recognition. The guard paced slowly up and down the room, gazing at the floor, tapping his ring idly against each hand-basin as he passed, missing out the two which Manning and Konstantin were using. Without hurrying Konstantin dried his hands, and went into one of the lavatory cubicles on the other side of the room.

Manning finished shaving as quickly as he could, cutting himself messily, and asked the guard for permission to use the lavatory. The man nodded, without ceasing his patrol. Manning locked himself into the cubicle next to Konstantin's, tore off a piece of toilet paper and scribbled on it:

'Kostik! You're safe! How did you know I was out?'

He dropped the paper over the partition and waited. He waited for what seemed a long time. The tapping of the ring against the basins began to sound impatient; he became frightened that the guard would order him out. Then Konstantin's hand appeared over the top of the partition, and a sheet of toilet paper fluttered down. It said:

'1. Paul! My great joy at your safety and freedom.

'2. My humble thanks for your silence.

'3. A message I promised I would deliver from Katya. She is out of hospital (it was hunger and exposure), but not well. Her mother has died. R. and I are looking after her. She insists you should know that while she was in hospital the police visited her and asked her about you. She told them you had deposited the books at the Kiev Station, and she asks your forgiveness.

'4. R. and I – both all right. Knew about you through R's father.'

The guard tapped on the door of the cubicle.

'Finished?' he said.

'Coming,' said Manning. In great haste he tore off another piece of paper and scribbled:

'Tell K. police would probably have known anyway. I kiss her feet and ask her forgiveness for involving her. My love to her, to R., and to you, Kostik.'

He dropped it over the partition. Then he put Konstantin's note in the lavatory pan and flushed it away.

39

The stubby silver Tu-104 screamed and shook, straining against its wheel-brakes. Dust and scraps of paper on the apron fled back from the blast of its jets. Manning pressed his face against the vibrating window glass, trying to make out Sasha or Konstantin among the scattering of spectators. But the only person he could distinguish for certain was one of the police escorts watching discreetly from a doorway.

He gave up trying to see and felt the shaving cut on his neck. It was still wet. He would arrive in London with blood on his collar. London . . . the name sounded as strange and promising as Samarkand or Valparaiso. Was the same brilliant summer's day just starting in London? Would anyone know he was arriving? Would his mother have been told about him?

The engine note rose. Suddenly Moscow, and all its cares and heavinesses, seemed remote and insubstantial. He had an almost physical sense of the city and his life in it as being behind him. For the first time he began to take in his sudden liberty.

Then the engine note fell again, and each engine in turn was switched off.

A great silence fell. Manning could hear passengers making small interrogative noises to each other. He had a sensation of falling. And only at that moment did he really appreciate the true quality of the nightmare from which he had just been delivered.

The steps were wheeled forward again, and the door of the plane was opening. Manning strained to see what was happening, but he was on the wrong side of the cabin. There were voices. Then the noise of someone coming swiftly up the steps, and pretending to pant, as if to demonstrate that he had hurried.

'Don't worry,' said the voice of one of the stewardesses.

The door was shut again. One by one the engines started and rose to a scream. And down the gangway in the centre of the cabin came Proctor-Gould, grinning guiltily, peering round to find a seat, and too confused to see.

Manning waved at him wordlessly over the noise of the engines. For a moment Proctor-Gould didn't take him in. Then his face came over red, and he shook Manning's hand with curious formality, and when he had finished, pulled desperately at his ear. They mouthed incomprehensible questions and answers to each other. Manning pointed at the empty seat next to him, and mimed doing up his safety-belt. Proctor-Gould sat down vaguely, for once apparently left at a loss by the progression of events.

After the plane had started to taxi, and the engine noise had fallen a little, Proctor-Gould shouted:

'Where did they put you?'

'Somewhere out beyond the Yauza. I'm not sure exactly.'

'I was in Vladimir. We had a nightmare ride in this morning – eighty miles an hour all the way.'

The plane took off and climbed into the perfect sky.

Manning looked out of the window. Already Moscow was disappearing into the ground haze behind them. He could just make out some of the skyscrapers – the Ministry of Foreign Affairs, the Leningrad Hotel, the University.

'Were you treated all right at Vladimir?' asked Manning.

'Not too badly, as a matter of fact.'

'Did anybody ask you any questions?'

'It was nothing but questions. I was interrogated almost every day.'

'What did you tell them?'

'Everything, Paul. It would have been insane to try and prevaricate at that stage. I take it you did the same?'

'No one asked me, Gordon. Apart from the warders, no one came near me all the time I was inside.'

Proctor-Gould looked at Manning rather strangely, the suggestion of an embarrassed smile forming about his lips.

'You mean, you haven't heard the details?' he asked slowly.

'Sasha filled me in on the way out to the airport.'

'So you know what they found in that book?'

'Yes.'

The stewardess was hovering over them, offering them glasses of tea. Proctor-Gould opened his brief-case and took out a tin of Nescafé.

'I wonder if you would make me up a cup of this instead?' he asked the stewardess. 'One teaspoonful in boiling water, if you would be so kind.'

'Like old times,' said Manning, after the girl had taken the tin away. 'How on earth do you come to have it with you?'

'I managed to persuade them to let me have it in the prison. The police had impounded it for examination. I couldn't bear the prison tea.'

The stewardess brought the Nescafé. It would scarcely taste the same, thought Manning, not having been measured out in a Woolworth's apostle spoon. He sipped his lemon tea luxuriously, cradled in the noise and the vibration, and the odd voices of people talking, squeezed to that high, soporific unnaturalness that voices have in aircraft.

'To be quite candid,' said Proctor-Gould, 'I was rather surprised to get such a friendly welcome from you. I mean, I got you involved in all this business, without so much as a by-your-leave. Any apology I might make would scarcely seem adequate. Nevertheless, Paul, I am sorry – deeply sorry.'

'I think I'm the one who should be apologizing, Gordon. I said a lot of stupid things. I see now that I was wrong.'

Proctor-Gould gazed at Paul, his head turned sideways against the upholstery of the seat.

'Thank you, Paul,' he said. 'I appreciate that. I'm very touched.'

'It's almost certainly my fault we were caught, too. I told Katya about taking those books to the station. She told the police.'

Proctor-Gould frowned.

'Katya?' he said. 'Who's Katya?'

'A girl I know. Or rather, knew. You put your arm round her once, a long time ago. Anyway, I'm sorry, Gordon.'

'Never mind, Paul. The whole thing was my responsibility entirely.'

'I suppose this is the end of the career you'd built up?'

'I suppose it is.'

Manning closed his eyes and tried to take in his freedom by imagining that he was still in his cell, and imagining that he was only imagining being on a plane bound for London. When he opened his eyes again Proctor-Gould was still watching him dreamily from the cushion.

'Nice to be on your way home, Paul?'

'Yes. Why do you think they expelled us, Gordon, instead of bringing us to trial?'

'I don't know. Political reasons, perhaps – something in the current international situation. Or perhaps it would have been embarrassing to reveal who was implicated on the Soviet side.'

'Maybe when they discovered it was just a matter of getting manuscripts out for publication they decided to turn a blind eye. It's the sort of back-door liberalism that's in fashion.'

Manning realized that Proctor-Gould had lifted his head from the head-rest, and was looking at him rather strangely. The suggestion of an embarrassed smile was forming about his lips.

'You did say Sasha told you what they found in the book?' he asked awkwardly.

'He said they found some money in the binding.'

'He told you how much, did he?'

'No. Why?'

Proctor-Gould sighed and fingered the lobe of his ear.

'I was afraid there must be some misunderstanding between us,' he said.

He thought for a moment.

'I suppose there's no point in not telling you,' he said. 'You'll hear soon enough in London. Well, Paul, according to my interrogating officer, they found 30,000 dollars in the book, in thousand-dollar bills.'

The balance of probabilities shifted quite slowly in Manning's mind.

'Somebody must have written a real best-seller,' he said.

'I knew you wouldn't like it, Paul.'

'There were no cuttings, I take it?'

'Cuttings, Paul?'

'Of reviews. You said there were cuttings of reviews. . . .'

'Oh. No. Listen, Paul. I'm just telling you what the interrogating officer told me. I swear to you, I was told in London that I was carrying a few hundred dollars in royalties for a Soviet author That's what I was told. Now, I don't know, Paul, whether I was told a lie by the people in London, or whether those notes were put in the book by the

K.G.B. when they examined it. It *could* even be royalties, you know. *Dr Zhivago* must have earned a lot more than that. . . .'

Manning gazed out of the window and said nothing. It was warm in the plane, and he felt suddenly dazed and crumpled and sleepy. The question which kept coming back to him now was why he and Proctor-Gould were being allowed to return home. He couldn't get it out of his head that Proctor-Gould must have compounded with his captors. Had he offered to use his connexion with British intelligence on their behalf? But they would know that British intelligence could not use him again after he had been in Soviet hands. Or perhaps they hoped that the British might be tempted to make use of him as a probable Soviet agent, and therefore a channel through which they could feed information that they wished the Russians to have. . . . Complex possibilities of deceit and counter-deceit opened out in every direction.

Manning could feel Proctor-Gould's eyes on him, following his doubts. He continued to look out of the window. Somewhere down there in the haze were the Valdai Hills, and the headwaters of the Dnieper and the Volga. Soon they would be above Latvia and the Gulf of Riga, then the shallow fresh waters of the open Baltic. Down there – the sweet blessing of frontiers, setting some bounds to distrust and corrupt dealing. Up here, no end to them was in sight.